Inspiration is a Four-Letter Word

By

Ken Hanna

ISBN: 0-7596-8944-X

This book is printed on acid free paper.

1stBooks - rev. 02/01/02

Dedication

To all who need inspiration at some point in their lives!
To everyone looking for to-the-point support!
I dedicate any success I may gain from this
to all who have crossed my path.

To my Cousins ~
Always treasure what
life has to offer
Love
Jun 2008

Table Of Contents

Introduction

I think a great tragedy in life is that more people are not able to express their views, their attitudes and feelings, on life itself—at least express them so that others may be allowed the opportunity to benefit. The "published society" takes the attitude that, unless you are a recognized *authority* on a subject, your opinion means little to others and there is no value in having it printed. You have to have years of training and experience in an area before your opinion means anything. How wrong can something be? I will not deny that so-called experts do have a broader insight into those areas they have studied, but many times they pass over the simple, obvious solutions to problems and make them more complicated than necessary. Maybe that is done simply to be "published." There are many people who have clear and logical solutions, but they are never heard by the masses. On the other side of the coin, I see many people getting published because they are *already* published. I feel the public deserves better. Do they not have the right to hear from one of *their own*? Inspiration can be—should be—simple, uncomplicated, and to-the-point. Inspiration should be a four-letter word!

x

1. Why?

As I watch the candle burn, I sit in stillness and silence wondering where my years have gone. For some reason, I have suddenly reached a point which gives me cause for concern. It has just dawned on me that the majority of my life is over and gone, and that there is likely few years ahead. To how many people has that feeling come—and how often has it arrived too late? Why don't more of us stop when we are younger, "consider" our lives, and decide where we want to take our future? Maybe it has something to do with a sense of immortality. When we are young, we are indestructible! That "sense" is fine, but how do we know when we are young that we will, in fact, get old? Of course, we don't know.

Having a *feeling* of presumed immortality is fine, maybe even "healthy," but the fact remains far too many of us waste our lives. We have no direction, no apparent purpose, no "reason" for living. How many have said, "Oh, I'll do that tomorrow. There is no hurry!" Then, all of a sudden, there is need to hurry—time is short. What we were going to do tomorrow cannot now be done because tomorrow is gone. Now we must live out our lives with regrets, remorse, and discouragement for not doing more when the opportunities were there. I guess this book is my compensation for those same failures. There were many things I wanted to do but simply said, "Tomorrow!" Maybe I can motivate some to take a new look around and realize the sense of urgency. We are here to love, to help others, to realize our "purpose" and do something about it, while there is time.

Use your time wisely! None of us should "play" God, nor should we assume how long we have. We should live by what makes us happy, what gives us peace and contentment, and by whatever will not "hurt" anyone else. I have always been—or tried to be—*realistic* about life. Maybe the Capricorn in me (if you trust astrology) has had something to do with my attitude—

all that "sobering logic" I have always used. I have always felt our lives are predetermined. We can often control and affect parts of our lives; but, in the big picture, everything is preset. If we accept that, the concern is how we approach "living." We can turn tail and run. We can cower and live in depression. Or, we can resign ourselves, accept the fact, and try to do what we can, for whom we can, while we can. We have to realize we are *all* here for a reason. Some know it and some never learn it. Some are not here long enough, but that was their fate. They were taken "early" for a reason, but even they had an impact while here. So, obviously, the effect they left was their "reason."

How strange is this life! It is not strange compared to anything else, because there is nothing else with which to compare it. It is strange based on our ability to reason, to think, to imagine. Maybe those abilities are not all that good—maybe we could live "better" if we could *not* reason, or think, or imagine. The point is, though, we can, so should we not use those abilities in a positive way? Reconcile your fate, accept it, and make it work for you! The one thing in our lives we *can* control is our attitude. So, control it! Your life will become tolerable and acceptable, at the very least.

Here I sit wondering what lies around the bend. There is no worry—just anxiety and apprehension. There is no panic—just a sense of urgency. I want this to be a "motivator." Let these words make you stop and think. Take time to reason and imagine. Set this day as the start of a "New Future!"

My "out-of-the-ordinary" reason for writing this book—as well as my first book, *My Life and Times*, centers around my way of dealing with adversity—by writing about it. These books have helped my cope with setbacks that have occurred over the last several years of my life. My way of reconciling myself to problems, for many years, has been to write about them. Putting on paper what is in my mind has always helped me "deal" with adversity. I have suffered through the tragedies of death, of love lost, of lost youth and health, of friendships abated.

I would like to think my feelings, my thoughts, may help others somehow. Not necessarily a better insight, but a different view. Just as writing this has helped me cope, reading it may help you do the same. If there can be anything "positive" in a tragedy, I have tried to find it. That has not always been easy, but I think the secret is the attempt. Even if nothing positive can be found, the simple process of reading about it can possibly help the coping process—I sincerely hope it does!

My first book was a biographical approach to growing and what I felt as events occurred and how I dealt with them. It centered around one man's view on growing—thoughts of life and death—on friends, and on love. This book is an attempt to center on those major events we all must face, and how I feel we can face them.

The events I have had to face were not particularly unique. Rather, they were probably the norm—setbacks, if you will, that most people have at some point in their lives. I guess my initial reactions to problems would be considered *typical*—I would get mad, get upset, get depressed, get feelings of hate. When I was younger, I used the "problem" as an excuse to get drunk. Getting drunk would make *it* go away! Of course, that never worked. Drinking simply led to other potential problems— physical damage to myself or, worse, to others; and, certainly, the guaranteed "hangover."

All of us suffer, at some time(s) in our lives, from Self-Destructive/Self-Punishment Syndrome! If we are faced with a problem, a setback, we are *required* to put ourselves through a certain amount of misery. The extent of that misery depends on the severity, or significance, of the setback. Certainly, a "major" setback requires "major" Syndrome Suffering! That is supposed to help compensate for things going awry. It is our *duty* to suffer. Unless we allow the syndrome to take over, the problem was not important—we really did not care about the setback. Is that reasoning logical?—I think not!

Of course, we all have to suffer! But we need to learn to suffer in constructive, positive ways. That sounds like a contradiction in terms; however, it does not have to be. If we are going to have a setback, a loss, an adversity in life—and we *all* are going to—the first thing we must do is recognize it and *accept* that we will "hurt." Once we recognize it, that hurt can and should be controlled. But how?

I think most of us grow with an attitude that nothing "bad" will ever happen. Indeed, I suppose some are even taught that early on. The "bad" side of life is ignored—not faced. Ignore *it* and *it* will go away. Obviously, that is not only a ridiculous assumption, but it is also unfair. Life itself means change! Like life we are all different. We are all complex. We all change. What is today will not be tomorrow! What we are today we will not be tomorrow! It is simply a matter that, as life around us changes, we must also change—adjust and cope!

There are constant "minor" problems we all face—we get the flu; our car breaks down; the cost of going out keeps going up; we cut our finger; it's 98 degrees and the air conditioner stops working; and on and on. "Something" happens on an almost daily basis—life's *trivial pursuit*! Even though we often over-react, these problems are short-lived and, generally, require only minor Syndrome Suffering. They are here and then pass on. Adjusting and coping is significant—critical—when we have to deal with life's "major" downsides—death and dying; losing love; losing youth or health; children; success or failure; and anything that can have a long-lasting effect on our existence. I think all of us need to learn better ways to cope with these "majors," and to adjust in some positive way.

I hope my thoughts help, because I care. We are all frail and full of faults, and we need help and support. If I can be part of that help and support, then I can feel an accomplishment. My "need" in life is to help others. I have come to see that as my purpose here. I get satisfaction when I have helped someone. I get when I have given. This book is a *"given!"*

Why the Sun Will Shine

I look to the sky where the sun does shine
It brightens the day, helps the world be mine
The outlook I take when I first arise
Helps the day go by with no surprise

It gives the chance to face all strife
The opportunity to affect my life
To give to others or myself alone
Challenges at hand to succeed or bemoan

We are tested each day by a Force unseen
With temptations and options we must glean
As we are human and imperfect for sure
It is not possible our choices are pure

So the test of our mettle comes each day
When our choices unpure dim the Sun's ray
How we cope when adversity strikes
Challenges greater than dealing with likes

Life unchallenged is not why we are here
But our test will come from what we fear
We must face each day along with the Sun
The struggle goes on 'till our days are done

Would That There Were No Sun

What would we have were it not for the Sun

Would we ever know when each day was but done
Would the flowers grow and all the birds sing

When would Winter finally pass into Spring

Would we never feel the warmth of Summer's heat
Would not the hues of Fall and leaves e'er meet

Can life exist without that magic from the Sun

Would we see all of happiness fade for everyone
Would our eternal destiny be but to live in pain

Can forever darkness mean we feel life's cold rain

Would we not feel each other's warmth in our hearts
Would love in fact vanish and keep us so far apart

Do we not need to see all that the Sun does provide

Would that we could see when its ray does subside
Would but that the Sun did not ever for us shine

What Is The Promise

The sun, for us, may not shine each day,
For with blue skies are skies of gray.
We were never promised a life of peace,
Nor an easy way for our pain to cease.

What our faith tells us is meant to be,
Is continued existence for an eternity.
To live with Him while embraced by love,
And to pray for all from Heaven above.

Once we learn acceptance of our fate,
From life to death we can then relate.
That will make our life easier to live;
Then peace and love we'll learn to give.

If given a choice, choose love not hate,
For love will provide a life that's great.
When love's your base, you live at ease,
And an eternal life will be there to seize.

We're Here

Some of us are here with a purpose in mind
Some are here with only a goal to find
Some of us come with a need to give
Some are here desiring only to live
We come to life with a purpose all set
A reason to exist and not to regret

We arrive here but innocent and pure
And not knowing our reasons for sure
But as we grow and learn of life
We are challenged with joy and strife
How we react and handle these tests
Will mold our purpose for what is best

That best for one is not for another
We choose from choices one for the other
So how we select what we must do
Is an obstacle faced each day anew
We have to face as long as we're here
Each day's joy and each day's fear

Some of us accept and handle it well
Some simply flounder because they fell
So we must help them when we're able
To pick them up and help keep them stable
We all have a purpose for being here
Use your time well because life is so dear.

Why Are We

Who decided we would be?
How was that decision made?
Yet, here we are!

Are answers available around the corner?
Revelation of life will come to us—
Eternity with answers lies just ahead!

Why are we?
Ecstasy and peace are for what we strive!

* * *

When is judgment decided for each of us?
Has our life been preset—predetermined?
Yet, here we are!

Ask never why but why not—
Regard your life as what was chosen.
Expect no more than life provides you!

Why are we?
Eternal contentment lives within us all!

* * *

Worry not but let life "happen!"
Hope and dream each day you are here—
Yet, here we are!

Always remember the answer will come in time—
Regret not one day you have been given.
Elation and joy will raise expectations!

Why are we?
Experience and accept life—truth will follow!

Ken Hanna

Who Are We

What power created who we are?
How have we come to be?
Over time, did evolution just happen?

Are we here for a purpose or reason?
Resolve of that will not occur.
Every person who will ever exist will ask.

Who are we?
Explanations will continue to abound!

* * *

Why must our time end before we know?
Has predetermination full control of life?
Of tomorrow, will questions go unanswered?

As we choose to live, will death copy?
Reality of now will minimize the unknown.
Expect nothing beyond what you have!

Who are we?
Each time you question, life shortens!

* * *

Whatever caused us has the answer.
Hope is all we need!
Our purpose is not to assume—just accept!

Ask not who or why or even when.
Realization will occur but tomorrow.
Eternal life will have all answers!

Who are we?
Everyone accept only you are who you are!

Ken Hanna

Why Not

Why are we even here at all
Why do we think and try to reason
Why must our time be so restricted
Why does Summer always pass to Fall

Why do we carry love and hate
Why does the sun shine so bright
Why will nature's foliage always grow
Why can just living be so great

Why must life exist filled with pain
Why will day and night exchange turns
Why do all living things have to die
Why is Earth cleansed by Heaven's rain

Why is it fatal when hate we've got
Why should we feel love so deeply
Why is this life our testing ground
Why the obvious answer is—Why not.

The Challenge

Life's biggest challenge is—Life!
Good and bad are constantly around us
We are faced with immediate reactions
Hopefully, proper reactions, but not always

Satisfactory reactions make us, keep us, happy
The unsatisfactory affect us negatively
And negativism will affect our total being
Challenge yourself and never give up

Learn to work thru all the negatives
Recognize and accept them as they occur
That is your true fate for being human
Because we are all created imperfectly

Done intentionally to challenge our strength
But tested not just for those negative reactions
Our test deals also with the good reactions
Are we humble or are we condescending

To condescend today will only mean hurt tomorrow
Humility today will simply reap rewards
Dealing properly with success will make failure easier
Success in perspective will mold your total being

Remember, every success means a failure lies just behind
And a failure only means a success lies-in-wait
Deal with all of life with a positive approach
Reward may not be immediate but it will be there

Let your faith give you the patience to wait
Life's satisfaction comes to those with faith!

Eternity's Start Is Life

Our life is not measured by its length
But instead it is weighed by its strength
We are not judged by how long we are here
But our worth is deemed by overcoming fear

Our time has value for having been at all
So the quality of life is our only call
As death is final and is our life's end
Life is eternal if loving memories we send

Our presence here will end when we die
But our memories left is why others cry
We want our worth to live in others' minds
And what we were will let them truly bind

Make your life eternal by the good you did
It's the bad you face that you must rid
Work ever hard to keep love in your heart
When love is there your eternity will start

When Does Eternity Start?

Why is it so many of us make life so difficult?
We struggle each day—death's still the result!
We have to fight each obstacle which we confront,
And that day is wasted searching for what we want.

Why can we not accept whatever God has given us?
But simply live this life and in God just trust!
This life is but a fragment that He has allowed.
So live with that time and for it ever be proud.

Why not change to positives the negatives you face?
When looked at closely, they can be fully erased!
Then the time He allowed you can be lived in peace,
And happy will be your days as all pain will cease.

Each minute you hurt someone will reduce your life.
And that hurt will compound by adding more strife.
So spend your time helping—your life will grow,
As love and contentment in your heart will flow.

Complete contentment will let you deal with all pain.
And you'll see life's mysteries are clearly explained.
Your life will blossom when love is in your heart.
And when your end comes, your eternity will start!

Our Need To Question

WHAT of life and the pressure to continue existence
WHAT of death and the anticipation to renew our existence

ARE we here only to exist until our time next arrives
ARE we armed with the knowledge to answer life

WHY must we live this existence in blind expectation
WHY have we no indication of what is the next "step"

IS love the true answer to the unknown question
IS it our place to even question what is next

WHO will be there to meet us as we arrive
WHO holds the answers to questions we need answered

WHERE will we find ourselves the next time around
WHERE will we spend our term of assumed eternity

WHEN does our "eternal life" begin its trek to paradise
WHEN can we hope to find that all-consuming answer

HOW do we transform in order to complete our journey
HOW do we prepare "here" so we surely arrive "there"

What Is the Answer

The trouble with life is the end is unknown
All we know is our time is here and now
Nothing beyond this are any of us shown
The Hand that guides us not one knows how
How different this life if answers we had
How would we all have to redirect our lives
Would knowing the end make us glad or sad
Would we live the same from what we derive

It seems much would change in how we live
Most would plan based on what we have learned
Having answers would tell us when to give
When to take and to cope when we're spurned
The answers to life would make living so clear
The challenges of living would be taken away
Would life itself still be held so very dear
In fact our purpose for being would turn gray

Existence itself would be for existence's sake
We would be here but just from season to season
Until our end is met we would but give and take
We would not respect life there would be no reason
We cannot know answers to live life as we have it
For that is not the purpose for our being here
To have the answers means we could just quit
So live as you see it and respect that fear

Life's Challenges

Life offers to all of us tests and confrontations—
Initiated by God and in many forms—
Fashioned by Him for us to accept—
Experiences good and not so good—
Solutions for which we must search.

Challenges we must face all our lives—
Helping each other as is needed—
Always seeking the best answer—
Learning to accept the results—
Living our lives through all outcomes—
Eternally grateful for the opportunities—
Never feeling regret or remorse—
Giving to others and not just taking—
Excepting feelings of self-pity—
Saying thank you to Him for those challenges!

Why We Need Tomorrow

What, ere, we made from such deep thought
On wings of high-soaring truth had brought
How had we come finally to reach this end
That to know this life gave us to mend

We chose to reconcile our known fraught
That had been found from what we sought
To mend all those ills and forward move
Our questions answered the mystery proved

That time was seized and truth was caught
What we held in our hand was but taught
Now we see those answers we did not know
The unfolding of life's mysteries did flow

So moving forward to all obstacles fought
The rewards as gained were not for naught
Once answers there enclosed in our hand
Our future was secured as had been planned

The Value of Our Treasure

The value of tomorrow, for us all, is too late.
How we are remembered is determined today!
All our todays will be how others will relate.
"What might he have done," is not what they say!

The value of our life is weighed by what was done.
What we were supposed to do is not the measure!
The quality of that value starts as our life's begun.
The composite of our life makes up that treasure!

The treasure left behind is given a relative worth.
And we all leave what is a different amount!
That value's comprised of all between death and birth.
So everyone who knew us will be those who count!

But our value will vary by the number who knew us.
So none of us leaves behind only one total result!
The smallest value totalled is what should concern us.
And a zero total by anyone is the ultimate insult!

Add to your treasure every chance through each day.
Fill it with your nows for tomorrow is too late!
Your faith in tomorrow will see it become a today.
So your treasure's filled if you do not wait!

What Is God/Who Is He

We all ask what is God and who is He?
Is He someone Whom we are able to see?
Is He merely an essence in our mind?
If we would search, will Him we find?

Though in His own image were you created
This ultimate in life is why you've waited
To live with Him should be your certainty
And that in life can be your eternity

But why must suffering be a part of life?
Why must we be challenged with strife?
Must we hurt so as to treasure the good?
Would we live better if but we could?

You must live life as He willed to us
Appreciate your moments without a fuss
Be grateful for your time—good and bad
Treat life with love—be always glad

Is our destiny set to be ended here?
Can we start again with abandoned fear?
Does He intend for us eternal peace?
Will it be that all hate will cease?

Trust your faith tomorrow will come
Contentment for all—not just for some
Treasure your moments—eternity you'll see
Question not what is God nor who is He.

Think of Eternity

How can life be explained when Eternity we cannot
conceive
We do not understand life, nor do we all know how
to believe
However we came to be at all, not one can truly
explain
Why so often do the good die soon and the bad
remain

Could not life be cleansed were it only the other
way
Would understanding occur if we could but see the
way
But this life is how we found it the moment we
arrived
And that acceptance has helped those many who have
survived

Just live for your time as God chose to give it to
you
For that tomorrow will bring an Eternity you'll find
is new
Imagine Eternity as that time of contentment and
peace
A heart full of love as all hate and pain is finally
released

Envision your new beginning when it's your turn to
"live"
Accept that moment and gladly take what He has to
give
Anticipate Forever as complete happiness and
serenity
For this is when we learn of love—preparing our
Eternity.

Ken Hanna

2. Why Friends?

Accept the fact that you are here for a reason! No one has ever lived or will ever live who did not have a purpose for being here. The question we all have is, what is that purpose? For some, it becomes very obvious early in life. For others, it takes many years of trials and tribulations before the reason appears. And for many, it never shows itself. Out of frustration and discouragement, many of those people simply give up—throw in the towel—and convince themselves that they have no purpose in life. They see no "reason" for their existence. Their life is a wasted effort. How wrong and how sad it is for those who feel that way!

Our society has become so complex that it overshadows many peoples' purposes in life. We find ourselves measuring a person's success in monetary and tangible gain. We look beyond the person and dwell on his attainments. When will we again start looking at a person for himself, and not be critical and condescending simply because he has less and has not achieved what *we* thought he should achieve? That is certainly not for us to decide. Who named us judge and jury for everyone else? We bring the same problem on ourselves. We condemn ourselves If we have less money than our neighbor, or we have accumulated fewer assets than our friends. We even condemn them when they have more than we do. Money begets money! Assets beget assets! How sad!

When will we remember that the friendship and love we are capable of are far more important than all we could acquire. We cannot take tangibles with us when we pass to the next stage of life. But we sure can take our feelings. And none of us knows how valuable those will be. I think our feelings—the love and friendships we have—will be immeasurably valuable. They will be valuable and important to use in the next *stage of life*, and they will remain important to those to whom we gave those feelings. I think most of us want to be remembered. But will we

25

be remembered by the property we left behind or the bank account we had? Not likely! We will be remembered by the *type* of person we projected to others. Do you go to a funeral, stand over the casket, and say, "He left two homes, three cars, and $100,000 in cash"? I hope not.

We all need friendships—friendships to varying degrees but, nonetheless, definitely friendships. We *must* have at least one "best friend." There can certainly be more than one, but strive for at least one. Considering all the people with whom we come in contact through our lives, there has to be one—and very possibly more—who best complements our personality, our thoughts and feelings. When you find that person, hang on with all your might and never let go! If you find that person, do not sacrifice any closeness with others. Most everyone who crosses our lives has something to give us.

When we are young and growing, most of us consider it vital—of major importance—that we develop friendships. But when we are young, our "real" reason for obtaining friends is to be accepted by our peers—to become part of "the group." Many of us will even do whatever it takes to be accepted—often disregarding right and wrong. And if we are asked to do something we know is wrong, we do it anyway. Acceptance takes precedence over everything else!

As we enter adolescence, it becomes even more vital if we are to become part of "the group." I would venture that most of our teenage alcohol and/or drug abusers fell into those "traps" simply out of fear of rejection. What have you really gained by destroying your mind and body? Was that acceptance truly worth the price? Do the friendships (?) gained justify the cost? Before making potentially dangerous decisions, look around the corner, not just down the street. Those so-called "friends" will *never* be there when you need them. And do you really need *them*? They will always have an excuse—they will never have the *right* answers for you. They know not what is best for themselves—how can they possibly know what is best for you? At those times when you *most need* someone, you need someone who *really cares*—not one who will lead you further down. If you are floundering and confused, how can you turn to someone who is floundering and confused? What is to be gained? Where is the *real* help?

As we think of a friend, most of us automatically assume that friend is of the same sex. Men will have men friends—women will have women friends. And that is the "natural" tendency. But I think too many people avoid developing friendships with someone of the opposite sex. Society itself has the impression that you cannot have that type of friend—unless there is "something" going on besides the friendship. "People" assume there is a love relationship—a man and woman cannot have a "friend relationship" without there being *more to it*. I think it is very important for all of us to have a friend of the opposite sex. Someone we can talk to and confide in.

Those who are fortunate enough to develop that friendship gain immeasurably by developing a "real" understanding of the opposite sex. A man can put himself in another man's shoes and relate to him—and a woman can do the same with another woman. But a man cannot truly put himself in a woman's shoes and "think like a woman" "—and vice versa. With a true "opposite" friend, you get an invaluable learning experience on which to draw and gain better understanding. You develop an ability to better understand the opposite sex—to appreciate and accept—to recognize the differences and learn to adapt, relate, and tolerate. What a more tolerant society if we all had someone "opposite" with whom we could discuss our feelings and learn! What a purpose for which to strive!

Many of societal problems stem simply from a lack of understanding of the other person and a lack of *wanting* to understand. If only those two walls could be knocked down, how much easier life would be. Living with understanding makes life understandable—easier and tolerable. Strive for that "success" and other successes will follow naturally!

Our lives are comprised of experiences. Every day offers a new experience—maybe even a potentially new "friend." At the very least, each day offers potentially new acquaintances. Some contacts may not be pleasant experiences, but accept them, too. Our lives are predetermined. *Every* experience has a purpose! And every purpose is a part of our "life plan." Accept the distasteful experiences as an integral part of our learning about why we are here. Hold no grudge and hold no hate! Analyze the good and the bad equally. Each moment of our life is the beginning of the end of our life. Try to live each moment to its fullest. Recognize it—analyze it—accept it!!! Be aware. Hold those moments—treasure them—for recall when you need them. All our experiences with friends and acquaintances will be used at some point in our lives. Every moment has a lesson, to be used at that moment or later, but used, nonetheless.

Friend

For those of us who are fortunate to have a
　Relationship we hold with a special
　　Individual whom we treasure and
　　　Enjoy and just like to be with and
　　　　Not just use at our convenience to
　　　　Do what we want

From our hearts and minds to a constant
　Renewal of feelings and
　　Integrity without jealousy to an
　　　Emergence of hope for the future and
　　　Never-questioning faith to
　　　　Develop a complete understanding

From the depths of our souls to the far
　Reaches of our imagination we should
　　Instill a total feeling that will
　　　Endure all the tests of life and
　　　　Never feel the slightest regret that
　　　　Devotion is vital for survival

For any of us to maintain such a total
　Relationship with another person we must
　　Initiate an openness to that person that
　　　Every thought should be filled with love and
　　　　Not ever a doubt that could
　　　　Destroy what we have built with that
"FRIEND"

—Reprinted from *My Life and Times*

Ken Hanna

Find That Friend

I have had a plaque since I was small
Which, I feel, says it all:
"A friend is not a fellow
Who is taken in by sham.
A friend is one who knows our faults
And doesn't give a damn!"
A friend gives us total communication—
He gives us that forever-needed shoulder—
That shoulder to cry on, or
That shoulder just to help us hold our head.
He will give advice, but only if we want it.
He will just listen, but only if we need it.
He will do for us, but only if we can use it.
He will pray for us, but only if it will help us.
He will show us the way, but only if he can see it.
There are many with whom we will make acquaintances,
But possibly only one whom we will call "friend."
He should be counselor and advisor;
He will probably think just as we do;
He definitely will feel the same.
God will see that we are drawn to that person—
For our own completeness.
It is up to us to reach out and grasp that treasure!
We all need that person—
We need as none of God's animals need.
We have to have that relationship or perish;
Not necessarily physically, but certainly mentally.
And mental existence is as important as physical existence.
That "friend" will see that we survive mentally.
But, we are a friend as well—
"Friend" is a two-way road.
Remember, we are helping as much as being helped!
We will advise, but when he wants it.

We will listen, but when he needs it.
We will do for him, but when he can use it.
We will pray for him, but when it will help him.
We will show him the way, but when we can see it.
Our soul is fulfilled when we find that "Friend."

—Reprinted from *My Life and Times*

Friendships

Find that one who will blend with you
   Reach for that relationship so true
      Identify how valuable that friend can be
         Embrace that feeling beyond all you see
            Never take for granted that one you find
               Devote yourself to that one-of-a-kind
            Stand beside each other as each would need
         Help with strength in the advice you heed
      Initiate responsibility that will be maintained
   Pray your devotion to the other will be sustained
So as Friendship lives, so shall your life!

Love and Friendship

Can love and friendship live as one?
In fact, I feel it should be done!
With only one, life lacks full joy,
And much is missed you could enjoy.
The ultimate from life is to have the two,
But those who reach that are far too few.

We strive our lives to find that one,
And if we do, our lives are begun.
Life's as fulfilled as it can be,
Sharing each other for eternity.
Friendship alone will complete a desire,
And mixed with love we reach even higher.

Complementing each other is what they do;
Working together to make our lives true.
But is all lost if one might fade?
Are all plans dead you might have made?
If love and friendship are both real,
Each should stand by what you feel.

Friendship itself is meant for giving,
And true love is why we are living.
Blended together, and both as one,
Makes life's search complete and done.
Success in finding the one that's right,
And then hang on with all your might!

Friend to Friend

To be a friend will mean to have a friend
Something we need more of in this life
A combination of personalities to blend
Two together in good times and strife

A friend is not one who would turn his back
He is not the one who would ever run away
He will not criticize nor turn gray to black
Never will he condescend or let us stray

A friend is that one who will hold our hand
Or give us that shoulder on which to cry
He will know always when we need him, and
He will keep us going when we no longer try

We cannot get thru life without a friend
That special person so vital for existence
A relationship unequaled that will not end
Someone beside us to help fight resistance

So when all seems lost, that one is there
And we must be there for when we're needed
For with no friend, life will head nowhere
Our time's been wasted if signs were unheeded.

Love Your Friend

Learn what life is all about
Often complicated and confusing
Very much a continuous test
Exciting and forever challenging

You must rely on instincts
Others are there to help
Use them for support
Rely on their judgment

Find that person who is special
Rest assured he or she will help
Instill a sense of trust and caring
Enhance the relationship always
Never take the person for granted
Do love your friend

3. Why Love/Why Hate?

Love and hate—what do they really mean—what are they really about—what part do they play in our lives? Probably more has been written on the subject of love than any other subject. And there are as many interpretations of what it is as there are people who would try to interpret it. Presumably, love is what you want it to be. Those who have written of love, wrote of it as they wanted it to be, as they saw it could be, as they hoped it would be. Love, in all its aspects, is the greatest gift of life. It can give us an unmatched inner feeling—a feeling which can be openly shown through our actions, our attitudes. Love can even make us "feel" healthier—often to the point of healing. It can serve as a potent non-prescription drug, curing our ills when nothing else will help.

The exact opposite, hate, is not a subject writers address very often. Its very nature is the ultimate in unpleasantness. It gives a depressing feeling just thinking about it. Its sole purpose is to cause a sad feeling, a depression incomparable, a totally unsound attitude. But, hate has a place! We need to look at it and try to understand it as much as love because the implications are as significant, maybe even more so. Certainly, love or hate of "non-persons" is not devastating. I hate broccoli, but that surely hurts no one. And my feelings concerning broccoli do not hurt, depress, or upset me. I just do not eat it, and my life continues unaffected. "I hate John," (no one in particular) will definitely have a critical effect, not only on me, but on John and/or anyone else with whom we two must deal. The impact of hate has a snowball effect—it grows and spreads like a cancer. "Hating" another person will hurt us in the other aspects of our lives. If we allow hate to exist in our minds, we cloud our ability to *truly* love.

Nowhere is it written that we have to love everyone, but it should be written we hate no one. Through our lives, we will encounter many people whose personalities, feelings, attitudes will not blend with ours—that is as it was meant to be. But we should not hate them. The message is acceptance! Accept everyone for who he/she is, not what *we want* them to be. It is simply not feasible everyone will *mix* with us. Our mettle, our worth, in the long run, will be measured by our reactions to those who do not mix. Everything that happens, everyone who happens along, happens for a reason. Look for it—find it—try to understand it! Once you can learn to do that, you will find yourself on the way to an overall happier life—that is just the way it is.

These extremes of the spectrum, love/hate, can have everlasting effects when we use them too freely, or in circumstances when we clearly do not mean what the words represent. Our lives are comprised of combinations of experiences and acquaintances. Realistically, not every one of those can be pleasant or satisfying. Life itself is a challenge against those things we would prefer not encountering, but encounter we must. We cannot avoid the "bad" side of life. It is as much a part of living as the "good" side. It is very easy for us to make the most of the *good* things that happen, the *good* people we meet in our lives. But our real worth in this existence is how we handle the *bad* things, the *bad* people.

The first obstacle occurs in how we feel about ourselves. Those who do not like themselves will find life's challenges almost beyond handling. The initial goal is to determine your *self*. Why are you here and what do you see as your purpose? Recognize it—accept it—like it! Low self-esteem will block your ability to accept others for their worth. Low self-esteem will lead you toward the hate side of the spectrum. Only when you can accept and love yourself can you move to the love side. You can then accept others better for what they are and what they stand for. And if they stand for something different, you can accept that and not carry hate. The least of God's people has something to give. And the least of us is no less a "person" than the next!

But what happens when you identify what you feel your purpose is and you do not accept it? You want your life to be more! There is certainly nothing wrong with that feeling. When you think you have "seen" your purpose in life and you want it to be more, God has obviously added that challenge. Take the challenge—use it to fulfill what God *really* intended!

Now, what of love? If you believe in God, you believe in love. God means love—that is what we are taught. Does that mean if you do not believe in God, you do not or cannot believe in love? I think not! Everyone needs love. You must love to help the fulfillment of your life. Love's connotation is good, hate's is bad. How can anyone be satisfied living with hate? Keep love in your mind and heart. Let love control the way you live your life—the way you handle all the experiences you will have. When you do that, only good can come out of those experiences. Even the "bad" experiences will end up with something "good." Memories we will want to remember. And we need *all* our experiences to result in good memories.

We all possess the ability to love. How that ability is nurtured is strongly affected by our environment in growing up. Many people treat as they were treated. Abused children become abusers of their children—loved children become lovers of their children! The children in an abusive environment *think* that is "normal." They have nothing to compare; hence, they feel that is the way it is supposed to be. Physical and/or mental abuse has a life-lasting effect. It seems vital to me that our schools, somehow, address what our society considers a "normal and abnormal" environment—simply, mental and physical *beatings* are not acceptable behavior. Get the children to think and to ask questions. For each child we can "save," we have helped a future adult and his or her children. The longer it takes for a child to realize his abnormal environment, the more traumatic his adult life will be; and the more difficult it becomes to help him through his problems.

I feel the strength and success of our nation is dependent upon each generation's ability to understand love—to use love—

to rely on love. We need to set the stage. Teach love—in the home, in school, in church, in support groups, everywhere! Like any other subject we learn, love *can be* taught. Once taught, it will be used every time it is necessary. And every time we use it, we learn to rely on it. And we must rely on it. The foundation of our lives should be love.

God had given us the ability to think and to reason. Given a choice, why would anyone *choose* hate over love? Should not happiness be our main purpose in life? When has hate created happiness? Those who live their lives in hate are obviously lost through their early environment. They were never shown love, taught love, and never understood what love can do—should do. They see hate, hurting others, as how they are *supposed* to act— their purpose in life. Those of us who were taught love, and have a choice, certainly should never opt for the other. There is no benefit to be gained through hate. But think of all the benefits derived out of love!

Before you can truly love another, you must be able to love yourself. You cannot give love unless you have love. And you do not have love unless you have it for yourself. There are times when we all experience a dislike for ourselves. We need to recognize those times, identify what the cause is, and work to overcome that *temporary* condition. If you have low self-esteem, then do something about it. Do not just accept it! And never tell yourself that you cannot be better. We have the opportunity in this life to be as good as we can be. Since we know not how long we are here, tomorrow is too late to start.

There is someone for each of us—someone who is a "blend" with us. That person will not only complement our personality (our feelings), but he/she will help strengthen us against our weaknesses. And we all have weaknesses. Finding that person is far too often a difficult, possibly impossible, task. But we must look! The scope of our environment obviously restricts the "choices." And living our life with love absent is unfulfilling. We live incompletely when we have no one to give our love, nor anyone to give us their love. Because we must receive as well as give. Success in finding that someone!

Inherent in life itself is change. Our lives change, we change. What we are today is not necessarily what we will be tomorrow. That is significant in the cause of so many divorces. Our dreams today, our expectations of tomorrow, should be shared with the other. Our hopes, dreams, desires—our *needs* from life and for life—must match. Otherwise, the relationship is likely doomed. Share and communicate! Fulfillment in life is to have experienced "true" love. That person, who is as perfect a blend as we are fortunate to find, is out there trying to find us. When you find that person, hang on with all you have. Work for the success it can bring, the happiness it can provide. Nothing in this life is better!

Remember, though, the other person may change—may have desires and wants tomorrow different from today. Life itself, influences beyond our control, far too often will affect what a person yearns for tomorrow—temptations which are so strong they submit. And it often occurs in spite of anything we would do or not do. But, if your love was true, do not turn it to hate. Treasure what was! Keep the memories! A true love that was is a gift of life, just as a true love that would survive. Do not destroy those memories, those times you shared. True love lost is greater than true love never found. Life itself means love and to be loved!

Love

Let us see as we dream about
    Our desires and wishes and
        Very high hopes to achieve
            Everything we could ever want

Looking only at the present but
    Only wanting a happy tomorrow
        Vital and full of life and
            Empty of all hurt and strife

Liking ourselves and what we have
    Offering always to help when needed
        Valuing our treasure of life and
            Expecting nothing beyond happiness

Learning about all of God's work and
    Opening the door to better understanding
        Viewing all His surroundings with the thought
            Each of us is here for a reason

Let us however not forget there is just
    One thing in His creations for us that is
        Vast and magnificent and beyond understanding
            Even though its letter say it all.

—Reprinted from *My Life and Times*

Ken Hanna

Love

God gave us what no other of His creations was blessed with—
    The ability, desire, the constant urge to love and be loved.

When we speak of love, we are really talking about growing—
    About how we will mold our lives and handle "death."

Love encompasses all else.
    It is the skin that holds our life together.

It is our greatest gift.
    When we have nothing else, we can always have love.

Without it we lose our existence.
    When we lose our ability to love,

We lose our purpose for life.
    To be able to feel and have

Love is a fulfillment of God's desire.
    Without it we are but another of His creations.

Do not ever lose it or you are lost!

—Reprinted from *My Life and Times*

A Word of Love

Love is the word for which there is no clear-cut meaning
It has as many meanings as there are people who would define it
It has intrigued man since the beginning of time
Poets have rhymed their thoughts—authors have penned their feelings

And the meaning is still limited by the numbers who have tried
The enormity of the meaning is in relation to the population
And the possible combinations are only endless
We are all limited by the extent of our environment

The greater our environment the more potential combinations
I believe there is a perfect match for us all
And to varying degrees we all want to find that match
Many get impatient and are fooled by what they feel

Others never stop looking then realize their lives have passed
What is the key in knowing we have found the best we can
We must weigh the value of any dislikes we find in the other
Then evaluate the importance of the likes we have found

To those with whom we become acquainted there will always be dislikes
But the value of those only we can determine
Remember too there are dislikes in us by the other
Each must share with the other all those feelings

Communication early will save any heartache later
And that communication must continue throughout
Without it the match will falter and eventually fail
So love and share each and every day for success and happiness.

Life with Love

When love arrives you should open the door
There's nothing in life that is worth more
It's the greatest gift that is given out
And to the world you should always shout

Let everyone know of the gift received
The joy that love has truly conceived
In its splendor and glory it's without peer
If truly love there would be no fear

Happiness and contentment completely abound
And thru the world its feeling's renowned
So never deny it when it's at your door
Just give yourself because it asks no more

For life with love is why we all live
We have it in us, it's our need to give
You will become whole for all your years
And then can face life void of all fears.

Why Does Love Hurt So Bad?

Why does love hurt so bad?
How do I handle all the sad?
Yesterday we were, Oh, so glad.

Do I simply walk away,
Or do I fight to stay,
Ever struggling through each day,
Striving for what I wish to say.

Love can cause an awful pain,
On the time I use to obtain a gain;
Very aware the love I want to retain
Each day as I attempt to sustain.

Hurting as I sometimes do,
Using memories to get me through.
Remembering the times I've had with you,
That will keep my love for you.

So the hurt that I must feel
On a heart I cannot conceal,

Brings a need I must reveal
And a passion I cannot repeal.
Darling, my love for you is real!

—Reprinted from *My Life and Times*

Life Means to Share

What a lonely life without someone to share!
Sad times are common when another's not there.
To whom can we turn when we desire to talk?
What joy will come from just taking a walk?

Having another to share thoughts, hopes, and dreams
Is life's intent—what The Plan intended, it seems.
Why are we here if not to share what was meant?
What's the point when too late life's been spent?

Our moment's been wasted if we let life pass by.
How comforting with another when we want to cry!
To cry alone will mean we simply increase pain,
And we lose the chance to understand and gain.

It is our inherent need to have another in life—
To love when we need and to comfort in strife.
How many have lost and thought life has ended;
That the one has gone on whom we had depended?

But keep hope alive that another one does live,
Who is waiting to share thoughts and to us give.
So never give up looking, for soon you will find
Another to share what is in your heart and mind.

The Plan's purpose said that life means to share;
That the ultimate is to find one who will truly care.
So never stop the search, for success will arrive,
And you will feel so complete and totally alive!

Faith—Hope—Prayer

It is more than that strange sensation
When we meet that "special" person.
It is more than a parent's feeling for its child
Or the child's feeling for its parent.
It is more than that urge we have as we grow
Or what we feel each time we get something we want.
It is more than our favorite pet or food
Or more than our favorite anything.
It is more than what we feel for life
Or what we feel religiously.
Love is far more than a four-letter word
Denoting that unique feeling we all have felt.
Although it may take many different forms
It always takes the same shape—
That shape formed in God's eyes
And designed for us to grow with.
We must be able to use love
To fulfill our lives—to enrich our faith.
But we must be careful not to abuse love.
We cannot use love and sacrifice another's feelings
Using love in that direction will eventually destroy—
Destroy us as well as the other.
We should take love in the direction it is aimed;
Where it will strengthen us both.
To love means to sacrifice—
To know when to give rather than take!
The reward will come by simply waiting.
It may not come tomorrow or when we want it—
But our faith in it will be our guarantee.
Faith—Hope—Prayer
And love will be there…

—Reprinted from *My Life and Times*

Love Must Live

What is life when there is no love
Where is love when there is no life
Life itself is but mere existence
While love must live eternally

Love will feed and nourish life
And life will fuel the need for love
So live your life by seeking love
That love continues when life's no more

Recognize hate is but a cancer of life
A disease that will only destroy
Love will be the only curing serum
Realize love and hate cannot coexist

Your heart can only hold but one
So make what is the obvious choice
Love must live to have eternal life
Life as we know will die with hate

None of us wants eternal death
Destroy that cancer before it grows
Hate is what we must see die
While it lives the less will love survive.

Our Gift from Him

To follow the path of love is a long journey rough
And it is so easy to give in when things get tough

Love cannot survive if easy times are what we expect
It will surely die when the other's faults we reject

Complete acceptance of whom we love will make it last
So draw on all your strength for now from your past

How invaluable the past when you need answers now
For what you are developed by the past showing how

And when you feel love has truly entered your life
Prepare for the downside for there will be strife

But let joy and ecstasy completely fill your heart
For then that love will provide eternity's start

Know God has provided us with the ability to love
So use that gift He gave us all from Heaven above

Nothing's impossible when love lives in your mind
Being down is defeated and contentment you will find

Our gift from Him is the one gift we can give back
'Tho abilities vary it is a gift we should not lack

You can deal with all that life might confront you
Toss aside the bad and keep your love forever new.

Thy Hand of Love

T o have been touched and to
    H ave been guided with
        Y ou toward a destination

H oping for a journey filled with
    A nswers to questions we
        N eeded to fill our complete
        D reams of Heaven

O nly during that journey's
    F inal voyage to tomorrow

L oathe did we feel as we
    O vercame our remorse to
        V indicate our transgressions
        E ver to live with love

T he Heavens reached down to
    H and me my destiny and
        Y ou comforted my sorrow

H ow often I felt in awe
    A nticipating what could affect me
        N ot realizing any consequences
        D ampened by rains of fear

O ften I strived for peace
    F eeling a sense of despair

L ikened to impending termination
    O ver in a moment's eye
        V ery strong determination to
        E ternity's cradle of love

Where Is Love

How can the feeling of love be described
But from words that are somewhere inscribed
Most of life can somehow be explained
Yet love's effect is a mystery sustained

Love touches all in a manner not clear
And the pain it causes can create much fear
We all search for what is our ideal love
Looking from nearby to the Heavens above

But love's not a place we search to find
It's an ultimate feeling—a state of mind
Love awaits everyone who wants its feeling
The ecstasy of it will send you reeling

It is unmatched by anything in your life
Its power can cure all setbacks and strife
Do not underestimate what love can do
And it's been always here—it is not new

Why are we so afraid of the power of love
It cannot destroy since it came from above
There is no denying that love carries pain
But pain is needed to see its power sustained

Your path in life will become much clearer
The purpose you have you'll hold far dearer
So find love and allow it into your heart
God meant for it as your eternity's start.

Let Love Enter

Love's essence on the wing of hope rides
And into our heart and mind it will flow
It soars to heights as an eagle glides
Nurtured by faith its seeds will grow

Not one is immune to the power of love
As it is spread to all by God's hand
Its strength touches us from Heaven above
When we feel its power as simply grand

Love lets us live through pains of life
It helps us remember the joys we've had
Love will lead us past all our strife
And give elation that will replace the sad

Life would be empty if love were not here
Existence to which we could not relate
Our hearts all filled with such great fear
And the dread that life ending be our fate

So let God's love just fill your heart
It will provide you with an eternal peace
And time-endless bliss will for you start
Contentment in Heaven lives as fear will cease.

Love Lost

The dark side of life, when reality strikes,
Hits when we are faced with love that is lost.
When love is real and we see a need to fight,
We struggle beyond what we think we are capable.
To save a true love is worth every ounce of battle,
But sometimes the struggle starts looking hopeless.
We continue fighting, watching for that ray of hope.
Eventually, though, we see the ray fade into darkness.
Wherever that love, it has vanished from the present;
Gone, conceivably dead for all time, not to return.
Now, we are faced with our remaining life!
Faced with having to continue into our final days—
Days into the distant future or just around the corner.

Lost love will overshadow all other problems in life.
Dealing with it is harder since it seldom happens often.
We have to react by our instincts and not experiences.
Well-meaning friends try to help, but mostly to no avail.
We appear to listen, but we do not hear anything said.
Everything told to us falls on deaf ears, but we listen.
We fault ourselves for not being what the other wanted.
We look back, trying to find an answer, any answer.
Mostly, however, there is no answer that can be found.
We are who we are, and they are who they are.
But we persevere, taking each day, one at a time.
Most of them we get through with little effort.

And then there are those which appear to never end.
Getting through is slightly greater than impossible.
But somehow even those days pass into our memories.
Then we strive to find a memory to overshadow the sad.
Sometimes fate plays a role in bringing what we want,
And the sad passes itself into a temporary void.

We find ourselves hoping to find an answer to happiness.
Occasionally, some of us find an acceptable substitute.
Something we think will replace the love lost.
It works for some and often will last,
And we manage to complete our remaining days.
For some of us, though, the substitute fails—
Fails because a comment, a gesture brings back the memory.

It all begins anew and our struggle recommences.
Every time it surfaces, our strength is tested harder,
And facing the remaining days is the ultimate test.
A rekindling, rebirth of love lost must come from the other.
After a time with only memories, we have to have a sign—
Some indication that maybe there is a new hope.
For true love lost we must keep the hope fire burning.
To see the complete fulfillment of our days!

—Reprinted from *My Life and Times*

What Should Love Be

Love is a feeling that is so hard to describe.
Man has tried forever its meaning to inscribe.
But its meaning will elude all who may ever try,
And the question we always ask is simply, "Why?"

If it could be explained, would life be understood?
Would existence be more peaceful, as it should?
The key to life's struggles is to identify love;
Then let its meaning surround you as if a glove.

Let love control the direction you take in life!
Allow it to determine how you deal with strife.
As you identify what love should mean to you,
You will accept your reason for being as true.

Too many of us flounder thinking that life owes us.
But the reality is to be grateful and not to fuss.
The time we are given is so very, very brief.
How many of us spend time with hearts in grief?

Should we not just be grateful for whatever we have?
Is it so hard to spread love as a universal salve?
We must emphasize the effect that love will give—
For the effect will provide peace as long as we live!

The Road to Travel

Love takes endless turns during our moment
    of life on earth.
It travels endless roads affecting our lives,
    incepting at birth.
No greater power exists than that exerted by
    the strength of love.
Its origin is unknown, yet its home must be
    in Heaven above.
No other answer can be found, nor can an
    explanation be made.
The influence of love is so encompassing, for
    nothing would you trade.

Once you let its full power become a part of
    how you live,
Every facet of your life gets stronger with
    that urge to give.
So use your moment of life to let in love,
    and push out hate.
The that eternity you seek will be ready—
    a step above great.
To all who truly wish what it can give, then
    love is here.
For as soon as you accept it, your purpose
    will become clear.

Search for Tomorrow

When love dies, your tomorrow looks dark,
And life's reality will challenge you.
For the death of love will leave its mark,
And your faith is tested to see how true.

Few things will hurt as much as losing love.
Its pain's unbearable and only time will cure.
You look for strength and answers from above,
And all you can see is the way things were.

You hope the dreams you shared would be again,
And for the completion of those plans you made.
But that life's past and another must begin,
And yet it's so hard when you feel betrayed.

But know God will provide as he always will,
To lead you thru that pain to a new day.
He stands beside you as you climb that hill,
To see you don't falter but continue the way.

So search until you find the other side;
For on that side will be challenges anew.
Do not stop short nor try ever to hide.
Build from your past—make your future true!

Ken Hanna

Love's Insight

The one I love I totally love
The essence of my entire being
She came to me on wings of a dove
It's hard to believe what I'm seeing

The love that grew was not dreamed
Nor imagined as it is for most
When it happened I just beamed
And to the world I would truly boast

She is so precious I cannot explain
I've not the words I need to describe
When I hear her name I will not refrain
To tell eternity in stone I'd inscribe

I'd tell of warmth and softness to touch
Her kindness and insight towards me
The pleasure she gives is never too much
The joy I feel will last eternally

She makes me feel over ten feet tall
And seeing her I beam from ear to ear
From the highest mount her name I'd call
For the rest of my life I want her near

It will happen and of that I am sure
Because something this good cannot die
It is a love that is so totally pure
My belief in that is on what I rely.

Life and Loves

Our life here is but a fragmentation of time;
It is but a "twinkling" of what has been or will be.
Why do so many of us realize too late that we have all
        but wasted our share of the fragment:
We all have a device built in which would allow the total
        living we desire—
But the trigger to activate that desire goes unpulled
        until it is too late.
How can more of us realize our dreams into reality?
Courage and self-motivation is needed, along with the
        realization that we ourselves come first.
We must understand that we are here for a reason.
The question then is—what is the reason?
Many search aimlessly for the answer.
But there may not be one answer—
Quite the contrary, it is possible that each of us
        carries his own answer within.
If, in our final breath, we can be assured we fulfilled our
        dreams, did all we felt, without the slightest regret,
Then the "reason" is answered!
We have to enjoy being "us."
If we do not like ourselves, how can we be expected to
        enjoy this brief moment.
The failsafe to keep us from total enjoyment must be
        controlled—
Defeated!
As we attempt to satisfy our dreams, often we hurt or are
        afraid we will hurt someone else.
Many of us then suppress what we want—thus sacrificing
        fulfillment.
But is the sacrifice worth our loss?
Hurt comes with living!
Controlling the hurt comes from self-determination—

From enjoying ourselves and not letting those hurts
    control us.
We need to learn from our hurts because many of them will
    happen again.
Losing a loved one by death hurts the one left behind.
But we must convince ourselves that the death will give
    "Eternal Life."
And when our time is due, we can join that loved one!
So we continue our struggle through the remainder of our
    time here.
The hurt hardest of all is losing a loved one who is a
    loved one.
All of us at some time have wondered if life is worth it
    when love has faded.
Especially if the one we love finds another.
That hurt can be the greatest test of all.
As we grow, we pass from "puppy" love to "first" love.
Losing that "first" love can all but destroy us—alas, it
    has in fact destroyed too many.
But, with patience and determination, we find what should
    become our "lasting" love.
The fortunate ones then have only to live their dreams—
    and the dreams of their love—through that fragment of
    time.
Happiness and as complete fulfillment as possible to everyone.

—Reprinted from *My Life and Times*

Together Forever As One

T o each other, pledge your heart and soul
O ne day at a time should be your only goal
G ive and take as you each will interact
E ven sacrifice, at times, as you seal your pact
T est not the promises that each of you made
H ave faith in the other, lest love should fade
E ach of you will bring something to the bond
R emember, always, there is not a magic wand

F or love and respect set the base of success
O nly communication should be your means to express
R ecall your day of vows when trouble should arise
E xpress your feelings so that your love solidifies
V alue that treasure that God gave each of you
E njoy each other for the years are far too few
R aise healthy, happy children, but when you are ready

A nd give them the sense your love is rock-steady
S tay friends with each other for that is a treasure

O pen your heart to the other, the result is but pleasure
N ever allow others to interfere or inject in your lives
E ternally know that your love but survives

Ken Hanna

Heaven Is You!

How often we seek true love
Each of us needs so much.
As we search and try to find
Very anxious for true love's touch.
Even when we think it's lost
Never to be found for us.

In life's amazing mysteries
Seeing its arrival to all is a must.

You came to me at a perfect time
On wings of love so true.
Until the end of my life on earth

!MY PRECIOUS LOVE, HEAVEN IS YOU!

Precious Love Eternally!

Putting thoughts into words
Relating to feelings
Elation abounds
Causing emotion to flow
Into a heavenly cloud
Our needs and wants
Under a shroud of desire
Send us to ecstasy

Living our dream
Only pushes us harder
Very greatly wanted
Entirely desired

Emotionally we need love
To share our thoughts
Enthusiastically live our desires
Recognize our limits
Never looking back
And ever striving forward
Looking for contentment
Longing for bliss
Yet always loving

!THAT PRECIOUS LOVE!

The Epitome of Love

I sit in the loneliness of my world
And I think about the times that were.

I ponder thru dreams of happy days
Thru thoughts of perfect moments spent.

The love we shared was as I dreamt
We two together were just as one.

Friendship that blossomed beyond imagination
Love conceived by His blessed hand.

But time and distance have altered feelings
Her desires and wants have changed.

What she said she wanted has waned
Her direction has gone to other goals.

The dreams we had are now only dreams
Dreams we envisioned together in our minds.

Thoughts of what we desired for the other
She knew me better than I knew myself.

What I was thinking she always felt
She would react and know what to do.

How I miss being myself with someone else
There is no one to whom I can give.

It feels what I have will die with me
She chooses not to hear me anymore.

She cares not for the feelings I have
Time for me is no longer available.

What she has to give she gives to another
One who truly does not appreciate her.

Whatever the relationship she says she is happy
And that is all I ever want for her.

I cannot carry hate in my heart
But I will always carry the memories.

No one can take away what I feel
That is mine to treasure forever.

Who can anticipate what tomorrow will bring
Live with hope that may come to pass.

I want her to always have what she wants
And especially to want what she ever has.

My feeling for her has gone beyond love
It is and will always be—Love Epitomized.

God Will Give Me a Tomorrow

I have lost my love and now I am lost!
Where will I go and what will I do?
Do I sacrifice life, the ultimate cost?
Will I give up or start my life anew?

The pain is a hurt that is so great.
To function happily is extremely hard.
God, what is to be my remaining fate?
I see not tomorrow, gone is the reward.

I saw my life as set and devoted to her.
My destiny appeared as she entered my life.
That life I saw so clear is now but a blur.
It seems I am doomed to live with strife.

God, where is it I am to go from here?
What new plan have You mapped out for me?
Without a clear view, I will live in fear.
How long do I suffer, will I ever be free?

Now more than ever it is strength I need!
Again I must overcome this living in pain.
"God will give me a tomorrow," is my creed!
Embrace faith and hope, and fear will wane.

The faith I have must see me through this.
My hope in tomorrow must keep me alive.
To see my tomorrow means I have to resist.
Life will be better and I will survive!

Forget-Me-Not

With petals blue, like azure skies,
    Waving with the breeze
So like the soul, that never dies
    To live eternities.

I pluck this beauty from its earth
    For all the world to see
This gift from God, blest from its birth
    Will live eternally.

Forget-me-not, a beauteous sight
    As sturdy as can be
Not even time, in all its flight
    Outlives eternity.

So grace this world, with beauty rare
    For mankind, such as we,
On earth, in Heaven, everywhere
    In blest eternity.

4. Why a Child?

The gift of life is love—a gift of love is a child! Wha greater gift could come to us than an extension of ourselves! saw the results of a survey questioning what people considerec the most traumatic event they could experience. Ranked firs was the death of a spouse—second was the death of a child Either some of those responding did not have children, did no realize the gift of a child, or simply considered their spouse more important. For those who never had a child, certainly the deatl of a spouse would rank first. But I feel that everyone shoulc realize that if a child exists, that death should rank second tc none. Even those who have never had a child should recognize that "special" gift of love. The loss of anyone we love is traumatic, to say the least. But how can the death of a "true part" of ourselves rank below anything else that might happen in our lives?

We experience many things throughout our lives, but nothing could compare to the eventual culmination of an event created, hopefully, out of an act of love. Unfortunately, though, that is not always the case—only what should be. A child is the blend of all we are, with all that our "lover" is. How can anything greater be created? It cannot!

Regardless of how that child was conceived—out of love or otherwise—we owe it all the love and care we can give. We are responsible for all the caring, teaching, and molding we have to offer. If that child is to live as an extension of ourselves, would we not want it to be the best representation and continuation of us we can make it? We must provide it all the values we have to offer. The groundwork laid in the first five years of life will represent the foundation on which that child will grow. And our responsibility is to build as solid a foundation as we can. We owe our child a foundation on which it will develop into a loving and caring adult. And the benefits will be returned—what we teach we also learn! It can only be a reflection on us, as well as molding another person of whom God can be proud. Simply do the very best you can, as in all the facets of your life. That is all God would ask—that is all anyone should ask.

We are solely responsible for bringing our children into this life. And they enter completely pure, totally innocent, of anything "bad." For all they know, once here you are here for good. Do we not owe it to them to explain the rest of the "full circle"? Is it fair that we let them continue believing what we know is not part of life? I think not!

Children are born with an innate ability to deal with and overcome tragedy, as long as they have some amount of understanding of the meaning of tragedy itself. We must also be aware that some children may not raise questions until after-the-fact. If we have observed our child's development closely, we should be able to identify that time when he/she is "ready" to hear about tragedy, preferably before a tragedy occurs. So, if nothing tragic has taken place and we feel the child is ready to understand in simple terms, then take the time to talk about it. Try to address tragedy before-the-fact. That is the ideal. Then, if and when something would happen, we are better prepared—they are better prepared—because the basic groundwork has been laid. Now we can personalize the event and take it to the next step. The child can then better reconcile and adjust using the knowledge that has been planted.

Early on, we should be taught that life is not always "great" or permanent. There is a "bad" side to life—no one is here forever; grandma and grandpa will die; mom and/or dad will leave (die or otherwise) someday; our favorite aunt or uncle will die—common potential tragedies to all of us. I think we are wrong and are hurting our children when we try to shelter them from the possibility of losing someone close. And when they raise the question of dying, we have a duty to explain it—in short, simple terms, but terms that will satisfy them and help them understand—given their age and maturity. I will not profess to know what should be said. That is as individual as there are people. But we must tell them something. It is a significant mistake to avoid the question. When a tragedy would occur, they would have a very difficult time dealing with, adjusting to, and understanding the meaning of what has happened.

Help them grow fully! If you are religious, then give a "God and Heaven" explanation. If you are not religious, then explain in terms that you do believe. The important thing is that you do not avoid the question.

Once our child starts school, our influences become secondary. He or she begins the path of individualism. What he will develop into will begin its formation. Our child is a *totally* dependent person the first few years, so what we instill becomes the base with which all else will mix. Do we not owe the child a base that it can draw upon in order for all mixes to become palatable, tolerable, understandable?—a base it can use to determine what is best and what is not. A child can only draw on its own experiences, and those immediately surrounding it, in formulating its purpose in life and what it sees itself becoming. Our children are the future and so are their children. So why not secure the future? As God intended, the future is secure only through love! And that gift of love lives within our children. So receive the gift that is there.

The gift of a child is not there for everyone. As we all have a reason for being, a child may not be in the Plan for all of us. The responsibilities and challenges of bringing a child into this life are not a purpose intended for everyone. Their gift of love will come in other ways. So do not condemn them. Of all the decisions and choices with which we are faced in our lives, having or not having a child would certainly be the most important. Nothing *should* compare to the decision to create life! Therefore, early education is critical in helping to prevent our young from the potential disaster of creating another life before they are emotionally ready themselves.

An "unwanted," premature pregnancy will not only alter the lives of the boy and girl, but will create a life-long trauma on that "unwanted" child. That child is the one who will face a possible life of despair and emotional upheaval. Is it fair when we do that to a perfectly *innocent* life? God gave us the ability to control ourselves, emotionally and sexually (something He did not give to His other creatures). We must be taught, however, of the alternatives and consequences when we find control difficult. A little education goes a long way in helping our young to grow as God intended. If you have a child, communication is critical. And it is critical when that child is a child. How can a young person be expected to understand the enormity of raising a child when he or she has yet to "find" himself herself? Obviously, that *must be* conveyed as early as possible.

What do we do if our child "errs"? Do we turn our backs? If we have taught love and we have love, then we cannot turn our backs. As best you can, accept the "error" and give whatever positive support you can provide. Be there when *your* child needs you most! If you have difficulty dealing with the situation, do not be ashamed to seek help—from a friend or relative, or from a professional. There is more and more help becoming available and just waiting to be used. At the very least, talking with a friend often can help us "see the way." After all, what are friends for if not to be there when we need them? Wouldn't we be there for them?

To have or not to have children—that is the question. Judge not the answer and condemn not the decision! Learn and accept—first, yourself, then all others. Once done, life will be rewarding and complete, and happiness will follow.

71

Children

Cherish the moment of conception to
Help bring that ultimate joy
Into your life with everlasting
Love
Dealing with the poor and the
Rich times they give to us through
Experiences shared with each other and
Never forgetting their unequaled gift

Challenges are the greatest tests we
Have in raising a child and are
Important in our own growth through our
Lives
Doing the best we possibly can
Regarding their development and
Education of life and love but
Not letting them stray unprepared

Completing the cycle of life through our
Help and guidance will help
Insure their continued growth and
Leave an impact on them of
Devotion and dedication needed to
Regenerate our purpose in living an
Enriched and rewardingly complete moment here
Necessary in preparation for "tomorrow"

Here We Grow Again

Kids are great but they can drive you crazy
It's God guard so we won't get lazy
They test you each day, it's their goal in life
They know how to work husband against wife
They enter this world not knowing a lot
But they come fully equipped to lay a plot
They learn early on how to work Mom
And she never knows where they're coming from

But the biggest pushover is dear old Dad
They know how to melt him when he is mad
They learn first off how far they can go
And what they can do so you won't say "No"
The world's greatest actors, rely on that
They can perform at the drop of a hat
When they are small the joy never ends
As they're asleep and when playing with friends

They look to us to love and protect
And we must give those and never neglect
Then they start school and we start to fret
'Cause all we have taught they quickly forget
Dads play ball with their daughters and sons
They teach them to catch and hit home runs
Moms drive to games and in car pools
Cook, clean, work, and even use tools

Kids then become teens and dating will start
On that we are "dumb" and they are smart
So we "suffer" through loves, we hope they survive
And they choose the right mate while we're alive
Finally they settle and are no longer wild
Then they bless us with a grandchild
We think back—where have all those years been
Oh, Well!! Here we grow again!

Ken Hanna

What Are Children

Oh, what a pleasure our children can be
The joy they spread is for all to see
But they will test us at every turn
Testing patience 'til they see us burn
They learn early on how far they can go
What they do is based on what we show
They push our buttons each chance they get
Then watch how we jump and never forget
They observe us when siblings are there
Do we show preferences or are we fair

Oh, what a pleasure our children can be
They are a joy to watch as they run free
They play always hard and sleep the same
And while they're small, life's but a game
As they grow, we see their choices vary
With their options changing, we get wary
Our concern is now their choice of friends
Do the means they use justify assumed ends
Has our influence seemingly gone from their minds
For all we taught, have they become blind

Oh, what a pleasure our children can be
If but they could stay small eternally
The pressure of peers will get stronger
And their time away from home gets longer
Puberty enters and their life's been changed
Love takes over—their future's rearranged
New problems for us are there to worry about
We try to help, but all they can do is shout
They are "love experts"—instead of I it's we
Oh, what a pleasure our children can be

A Gift of Love

There is no greater gift of love
Than a child sent down from above.
A satisfaction of that we dream,
A culmination upon which we beam.

Love's result that becomes real
The sense only a parent can feel.
No feeling in life can be as great
It carries an insurmountable weight.

Treasure the moment when it would come
Hold it close and do not ever run.
Give it all the love you possess
As a base on which it will progress.

For the love you give it gives back
And see how precious is that fact.
Covet that child with all your might
You will beam brighter than any light.

Life's Purity and Innocence

God's purest gift in life is a child.
It "arrives" completely pure—completely innocent.
At conception, there is a blend of the parents—
An unknown mix of all that represents their make-up.
When born, a child is as innocent and pure as it will ever be.
The rest of its life will involve a constant loss of that purity
and innocence.

That child, throughout its life, is at the mercy of its parents
and environment.
What type person it is to become is completely dependent
upon all that will surround it and influence it.
The stage is set at the moment of birth.
How long it will be here is already known—

Not to us, but to God alone.
Its contribution in life is subject to its time here.
And every person makes some contribution—
For some, it is much—for some, little—for all, something!
Life, then, represents how much purity and innocence is *lost*.
Nothing else in this life is as potentially significant as a child.

Every child represents a contribution to life!
Every child is as "important" as every other child.
Do not weigh the contribution alone.
Accept only that there will be a contribution.

Ken Hanna

Life itself is enhanced by every child born.
Our purpose should be to try to minimize our child's loss of
     purity and innocence.
We must protect it from "bad," but also teach it to recognize
     "bad."
We must help it set its foundation through love.
The stronger that foundation, the better its life.
And the better its life, the less purity and innocence will be lost.

   We owe that to God's Purest Innocent!

Life with Children

Children are here with a mission in Life
To cause us aggravation and create strife.
They are the supreme testers of how good we are
In coping with them whether in peace or at war.
We must treat them with love and also respect
Challenge their abilities, not what we expect.

Stand by them when up or when they are down
Be their strength if they are wearing a frown.
Recognize they are different, not the same as us
They're born with our values so don't cause a fuss.
Teach them to stand on their own two feet
How to handle success and deal with defeat.

Never condescend whenever they succeed
But be humble as thru life they proceed.
Teach them to care about their fellow man
That is the basis of God's Master Plan.
Be grateful for whatever comes their way
They should hold no jealousy and never stray.

Keep love in their hearts and do not hate
It is what life intended as our fate.
As roadblocks come understand what is meant
Persevere thru life and never relent.
Accept the bad with good, it's what is planned
Then Life will be tolerable and definitely Grand!

79

"Man" of God

Husband, father, brother, and son
Man will live each day as one
His role will change as is required
To be one or the other as is desired

As a son is how he will start his life
Before a dad, a brother, or taking a wife
He'll start to form the type he will be
Setting his standards from all he will see

As a brother his love is different still
For sibling love will his heart fill
'Tho friends may pass, a brother will stay
To be there when needed, you can always pray

As a husband he must always show love
To that one he has chosen from above
He must be kind, understanding, and true
To make her life each day feel new

As a father his test will be supreme
To see his children grow will make him beam
For they will live on when his days are done
Life's ultimate test, to compare there is none.

"Woman" of God

Mother, sister, daughter, and wife
Her instincts grow throughout her life
A woman develops that special sense
To protect and nurture with no pretense

As a daughter she learns what she'll need
To all those around her she will heed
She learns to live in a peaceful way
Dealing with others each and every day

Her role as a sister is a special one
It will not end 'til her days are done
To protect her siblings one and all
She sees her duty and answers the call

She becomes a wife and has a "new" love
From all until now this will stand above
She'll share her thoughts with whom she found
Her joys and feelings will greatly abound

She becomes a mother, the circle's complete
This "ultimate" love has nothing to compete
To bring new life cannot be described
For in God's mind it will be inscribed.

Life's Challenge

Life itself is a constant challenge
Each moment of each day is a test
God confronts us with obstacles
Obstacles to challenge our reactions
Some of those will be unwanted
Tests we would prefer not having
But necessary in living this life
No one ever promised a "perfect" life

That is just not a possibility
Life means having obstacles
As many different experiences as possible
We have challenges from the "outside"
And challenges from "within"
One of the greatest challenges is a child
A life extension created by ourselves
An image and composite of us and our mate

No wonder no two people will ever be alike
We can know ourselves completely
And our mate as much as possible
Yet we still know not the result of the union
The more we know the less we know
We must accept that "creation" for what it is
Another unique person through God's will
How wrong to try to make that child what *we* want

That child is like no other in life
Different from everyone who ever was
With a potential unmatched or unequaled
We owe our children an opportunity
A chance at developing their "gift" to life
At conception their gift is unknown or untapped

At birth it remains the same
It will not be known for years to come

Sadly for some it is never to be known
What they learn early will set the stage
What they learn can only come from us
Do we not "owe" them the best we can give
The better we know what life is about
The better the stage we can set for them
We owe our children as we owe no one else
They asked not to be conceived

Since we are *totally* responsible for their being
We are *totally* responsible for their initial development
We will lay the groundwork on which they will grow
It only makes sense to lay the best foundation we can
They are only in part examples of what we are
They are partial extensions of our being
As others see us in them
Let others see the "good" projected

Life's challenge is our children
Life's challenge is indeed great!

5. Why Grow Old?

What happens when we awaken one morning and suddenly realize we are no longer "young," but are getting older? There are certainly worse things that *could* happen; but, for some, that is a potentially catastrophic "event." Remember, though, given the full spectrum of this existence, each of us has only a minute amount of time here. We have borrowed—stolen—our *share* of that time. Our time here is predetermined, yet most of us know not how long that will be. How important, then, that we make each day "count"!

In some ways, those who become terminally ill have an advantage over most of us. God has chosen to take them, and He has *allowed* them to know in advance. It must be understood that it is for a reason. Everything is for a reason! And that is definitely no easy acceptance. There is guilt, depression, remorse—"Why me?" There is suffering, hate, self-pity. Those are all *natural* feelings. After all, we are *only* human. The sad part of life is when a "young" person is faced with a terminable life. We see that, above all else, as unfair. That youngster has not been given the chance at a "full" life, as we expect life would be. God is taking him or her "before their time." But is He? If you believe in God, then you *must* accept the fact He has a reason—He wants that youngster with Him. Your faith in that will help you reconcile what has happened. It will not necessarily ease the pain, but it can help you reconcile His decision. And are we not here to live out His purpose for each of us?

So, is youth wasted on the young? I think not! Youth is wasted when we choose to not "like" ourselves or our lives. How vain it is and how selfish when someone worries about "getting older." As long as we are *satisfied* with ourselves, and try to accept who we are, then "youth" is only relative. You have no control over aging chronologically, but so what? Using your time being concerned over something you cannot control is

84

wasting your time, and that "waste" will affect other facets of your life. Realize your purpose is in being here at all and what you do with the time you are allowed, however long or short that may be. Since each day is the beginning of your end, make it count! Do not preoccupy yourself with "getting older." Occupy yourself with, "I have another day to give—to contribute—to be! What can I do to best use this *extra* day?"

None of us knows the alternative to life. For all we know, this might be it. Hopefully, though, there will be something tomorrow—another life, another existence, another time. I think we all want that and probably most expect that. So this could be our preparation, our training ground, our test of how we will fare the *next time*. Make it the best you can! Consider each of your days as another chance to practice. And the longer you get to practice, the better you will become. But practice every day, regardless of how long you may have. Do not see yourself as "getting older," only better and better prepared. It has to be worth the effort, so make that effort! Create a feeling in your mind and heart that will take you in a "positive" direction—a feeling of self-acceptance and acceptance of everyone, and a sense of what God expects from you for your allotted time.

Following are several writings from *My Life and Times*. They are my feelings as I see our time here. I hope they give you "food for thought"—for accepting better who you are, why you are here, why there is life at all, and where you *might* be headed.

May you accept today, anticipate tomorrow, and know that in *time* you will get there!

Life

Learn first to accept your destiny and
    Imagine how you can shape your
        Future around the present by molding
           Experiences into lessons to learn

Let your experiences show you how
    Insight into their purpose can more
        Fully reward your life into an
           Exact fulfillment of God's desire

Lessons we must continually learn should
    Initiate a desire in your mind that
        Fulfilling your dreams is foremost and
           Expectations of your future vital

Learn to live each moment of your time
    In a way that you will enjoy your destiny
        From the time you realize that your life is
           Enhanced by your search for happiness

Live that life to its utmost potential and
    Instill in your mind an urge that will
        Finally lead you past all adversity so that
           Enjoyment of what you have is your "LIFE"

—Reprinted from *My Life and Times*

Life

How do we express our thoughts of growing, of life, of death?
   Thoughts we all have searched—worried about.
Many of us "wonder" but just accept them and keep going—
   Not asking and certainly not answering.
How do we cope with the adjustment of growing?
   Because we never stop and should never stop growing.
We must continually grow mentally.
   Good mental growth is vital, crucial, and certainly healthy.
As we grow, we wonder about Life—
   Who are we and why are we here?
Many find the answers for themselves.
   But too many search aimlessly and endlessly.
And never find a "satisfactory" answer.
   We all must search—
But we must accept what destiny we have.
   We cannot wonder about Life without wondering about death.
Death is a necessity of Life!
   We have to accept that ultimate end.
But is it really an end?
   A primary need of living is accepting death as a beginning.
Accept that with complete faith and Life will be fully rewarding.

—Reprinted from *My Life and Times*

Ken Hanna

What You Have Is Life

Some of us grow
And some just go,
Attempting to set a pace
That will get us thru life—
Not fulfilling our potential
And definitely not achieving
What could be more happiness.
We hit a narrow path,
Fall into a routine,
And eventually reach a point
Of being fearful of any change.
Many of us become material-conscious,
Actually believing our purpose here
Is the acquisition of possessions.
When we reach that point,
We have to be doomed.
Our lives are not rewarded
By a measure of material gain;
Our reward has to come to us
In the next beginning.
So we cannot stagnate our minds!
Our complete happiness,
Our full potential,
Must come from mental growth.
We must try to aim at our destiny—
Happiness achieved now
Has to give us a satisfying new beginning.
Our achievement today
Is happiness tomorrow!
Look for—seek—that which will give you
A greater peace with yourself;
A mind with happiness in it;
A heart filled with love—

Love for yourself and what you have;
And what you have is "Life!"
Carry love in your heart
And you carry life everlasting.
Just being alive and sharing that with others,
Loving all that God has provided,
Is the real reason we are here.
Consider we are in training now,
Practicing for our eternal beginning.
Do not waste this short time!
Use your capacity to love—
And you will be loved...

—Reprinted from *My Life and Times*

Ken Hanna

Moment to Moment

Each moment of time is fleeting
Here and then gone
Never to return to us
Never to repeat itself
Never to again be lived
And all-too-often, here and gone
Before we know it
So each breathing moment should be
Live to its fullest
We must take that moment
Grab it—analyze it—use it for all of its worth
For every moment is worth an entire life
A treasure greater than any value
A value beyond our comprehension
Since the moment now is not the moment next
The value of now is as great as it will ever be
Because in just a moment, now is gone
And will be the now that was
And the now that was cannot be lived again
We cannot live past moments in the present now
If we do, now will not be fully savoured
It will not be used for all of its worth
So it will be lost and we will be less
Less for not living it to its fullest
But more—each succeeding moment we also will lose
Because we should grow with each moment
Since that moment will strengthen us
And help us for the next moment
Live that moment today
And anticipate tomorrow
For you will have a moment you have never had
Nor will ever have again

—Reprinted from *My Life and Times*

Precious Time

Time flies when you're have "fun."
But don't forget an important fact of Life—
Time flies, regardless!
Our years are limited—our days are limited—
Our time is limited.
Predetermined and set;
Set by God for us to handle.
'Tho our time is set,
We ourselves must mold its use.
Since we know not when it will end,
We must carefully plan;
Getting all we can from each day
Since that day will not return again.
Get all we can—learn all we can!
For each day has a lesson to be learned.
If we approach a day and let it pass by,
We have lost, never to recover,
What God had intended.
And what he had intended was an experience—
An experience never to be duplicated;
Never again to return.
And we would be less than what He had planned.
We must confront that experience—
Even if it is not what we really want.
For the "bad" experiences also carry a lesson;
Maybe even more important than the "good" ones.
But if we turn our backs on those distasteful experiences,
We have most certainly lost a lesson
Which would have made us stronger for the next encounter,
Regardless of whatever it may be.
For the experiences we don't want to have
Are a test of our ability to cope and grow.
Facing and accepting those experiences will help us

To better appreciate and handle the "good" ones.
Because we will have plenty of good ones.
Anticipation and patience are vital!
If we want that life God has planned for us,
We need to use our "time" to its fullest.
Anticipate each day with all your zest and excitement!

—Reprinted from *My Life and Times*

Lessons of Experience

We are confronted each moment by life's challenges.
How we face them and react to them will determine how we
    will grow.
Because our entire life is a growing process
We must strive always to continue growing.
To stop growing means to stop "living"!
There is a point when physical growth will cease,
Except for outward changes that we have little control over.
But mental growth will never stop, or better, should never stop!
How do we maintain that vital mental growth?
How do we face all the challenges and learn from them?
How do we react to all these experiences?
First, we need to be able to look beyond the obvious.
We cannot ask ourselves, why me?
We must ask, what is it trying to teach me?
There is a lesson to be learned from all experiences.
Once we see the lesson, then we are ready to learn—
To better react and cope, and eventually,
To be more prepared for our next beginning.
Because God has put us here to prepare and train for that
    eternal life awaiting us all!
Next, we cannot distinguish between good and bad
    experiences—
An experience is simply an experience!
Good or bad comes from our reaction to it at that time.
A bad experience now could very easily be a good experience
    in another time or place—
And the opposite is equally true.
We must react objectively, as much as possible, to each and
    every experience, in order to get as much from it as we can.
Certainly easier said than done, but once we can understand
    that, it definitely will be easier.
Then, we should consider the experience a teacher.

Something God provided for us to learn from—
To develop from—to grow from.
For how can there be life without experience?
We are not here merely to exist, die, and go to the next
    beginning.
We are students—learners—in training for that beginning.
And to avoid any experience is missing a lesson.
So each lesson missed means we go that much unprepared.
Anticipate experiences for the sake of experience!
Look forward each moment to the next challenge—
    it has to be rewarding.
The more challenges faced, the more experienced.
And the more experienced, the more prepared!
And the more prepared, the better the next beginning...

—Reprinted from *My Life and Times*

Ken Hanna

Mold Your Experiences

Our lives are geared and molded
To a long search—
A search for identity
A search for reasons why
Why we are here and
How we will make the most of what we have
Will we survive the tests of life—
Will we become better for what we encounter
Or will we develop a self-pity
And become mentally inadequate
Our time here is short
We cannot waste even a moment
Every second of our lives is predetermined
To teach us and test us
We must accept this fact
And approach each of these "tests" with a foresight
With an attitude that there is a lesson to be learned
A lesson which God has provided for us
As soon as that fact is accepted
Our lives can be fuller and more rewarding
We can then go forward each day
With a better understanding
To comprehend why we are here
And where we are going
Look at each "test" with an open and objective mind
Accept the test for what it is
It has met us for a reason
Use that fact and learn from it
Our lives are molded from experiences
The mold is cast by how we use those experiences
And if that mold is to set well
Those experiences should teach us something
If we do not gain from these endless encounters

The mold will not take as it should
And it is all-too-often too late
To try to recast a new beginning
But if we learn as we should
Our mold will have been set
Just as God intended it should be—
Solid and strong—not a crack—
And definitely unbreakable
This is our preparation for tomorrow
Our preparation for the next beginning…
All the wiser for having had it
All the stronger for learning from it
All the better for just living it
For all experiences—good and bad—make living worthwhile
And the more experiences the more worthwhile is living
Anticipate experiences
Look forward anxiously to just having them
Accept all of them
Our short time here can only be rewarding.

—Reprinted from *My Life and Times*

Why?

When you're alone where is the joy of life
What is His intent with this added strife
Is His only purpose to change us
Or beyond is His desire more for us

Why must we struggle day by day
Is part of our life to be coloured gray
Must we be lonely when we are alone
Can our feelings change when we are grown

Time alone is time we all should seek
It is when we can weigh what is bleak
A chance to reconcile what is wrong
Try to accept it and then move along

Accepting only the good is not complete
Without dealing with bad when it we meet
God's circle of purpose covers good and bad
Having both we'll treasure what we've had

Live all moments of life before it's too late
And never mix good and bad with love and hate
He chose our understanding of bad through good
To love all of life whenever we could

Question not why He drew this existence
Deal with it all without any resistance
Cope and accept and you can then move on
This Life is limited—here and then gone.

Where Is My Peace

So still is the day ahead for me,
And quiet the night which will follow.
The pain is so great for what I see,
And my heart is empty and so hollow.

I question my life—where has it gone;
Why has autumn arrived so very fast?
How much longer will I see the dawn;
Do I have time or is tomorrow the last?

Few of us know when our days will end.
We're never prepared for what's to come.
What's happened before we cannot mend.
But our past is where our future's from.

At a point, we must look at our past;
We must see the bad and what was right.
Remember what was, so memories will last;
Your future then can be painted bright.

Fill your hollowed heart only with love.
Let faith take full care of your mind.
Let your winter peacefully flow from above.
Do all this and contentment you'll find.

6. Why Cope?

What I have been saying is that we have to cope with life from the moment we are born, and it does not stop until our final breath. Life is but a constant challenge. Every time we turn around, something new is waiting, ready to confront us, daring us to fold up/give up.

Early on, life is completely uncomplicated. Our major concerns, the only concerns we really have, are eating and sleeping, and getting our diapers changed on demand. The only people we have to deal with are our mother and/or father and we learn very quickly what they are all about. We find out how to cope with them and what it takes to get what we want, when we want it. And all the while we are "training" them to cope with us. If there are siblings, we do the same with them. We enter this life totally self-centered. Nothing matters except our own well-being. All in all, it is a very simple life—no complications, no *real* problems. And yet it represents our first challenges in living with others.

The next stage will generally involve learning to "live" with those outside our family. During those first couple of years, we are completely selfish—the whole world centers around us. Only *we* matter! Hopefully, we are *taught* about the feelings of others—that *they* matter, too. It is something we have to learn. This will be the basis for how we treat others throughout our lives. We learn how and when to put our wants and desires second. School will give us our first real *taste* of this "problem." We are placed in a captive situation with others our age, as well as some older and some younger, some we may know and some we do not know. This situation is under the control and direction of a "new" authority—not our parent or anyone we know. Nonetheless, we discover it is someone new we must obey— *orders* not from home, but *orders*. All of a sudden, our test of coping with authority, learning to take directions—being told what or what not to do—and having to do something that we

100

may not wish to do, enters our lives. And yet this is still a relatively uncomplicated part of life, compared to what is yet to come.

Eventually, and without fail, puberty hits! We change physically and emotionally. Boys start seeing girls in a different "light" (something girls had already been doing regarding boys). What is this strange attraction to the opposite sex? We have not experienced this feeling before. Our lives are never to be the same again. This "new" challenge involves finding that person we have an urge to be with and who wishes to be with us. But, because life is not easy, most of us are constantly faced with "snags." The one we want may want someone else. And they, in turn, may want another, and on and on it goes—the dating/mating scene—trying to learn how love works. Experience for many of us is limited, so when we do not *get* the one we want, we are "crushed." Even worse is the devastation we feel if we get that one and later they choose to move on to someone else. That "first love" lost is traumatic. At the time, we see it as the *end* of our "love life" (for some, sadly, it represents the end of life itself). There cannot possibly be anyone in this life whom we can "love," and no one can tell us any different. But this strange life does provide! Accept that fact. You will live through the *hurt*. Recognize that it is just the tip of the iceberg. Coping with love is life-long. See it as one of life's challenges, nothing more. For some, it may be the biggest. For some, it may be insignificant. For all, it is just a part of life!

If and when "the" love arrives (and you will know it), be prepared to accept one of your major challenges. But do not fool yourself—it is not a 50/50 challenge. It is 100/100! Both must give all they can to make it work, make it last. Most of us are weak, though, and sometimes a loss of effort from either or both will cause love to fade. Sadly, love sometimes changes colors completely and becomes "hate." When it changes extremes, there must not have been "true love" in the first place. There should *never* be hate. Hate will destroy! Accept the experiences you shared. Be grateful for having lived them. Keep them positive in your mind—learn from them. Cope and continue!

None of us are immune to coping with death. Sometime in our lives we must face dealing with the death of a close relative, a spouse, a child, a friend or acquaintance, or a love. It is easier for some, but it is not easy for anyone. At an extreme, some cannot deal with death at all. It is so tragic, they end up taking their own lives. So sad and yet it happens. They needed help and either had no one to look to, or the wrong things were said, or nobody spotted the warning signs of a problem. We must all learn that death is part of life—simply a stage, an extension, of living. God had a reason for "taking" that person; otherwise, they would still be with us. Your *faith* in God should help you reconcile the fact, accept it. Death is a tragedy only to those left behind. If you believe in God, you know we live only in preparation for eternal life with Him. If you do not believe in God, you reconcile according to what you do imagine. We all must believe in something—it is our strength in living *this* life. Belief in nothing means we are simply floundering through this existence. I doubt there is anyone who *really* wants to think this life is it. Everyone has a conscious or unconscious desire to "live" after death. I don't care who they are. Given that, coping with death can be more tolerable. Cope and accept!

Each and every day of our adult lives entails coping with society and surviving. We have reached a point in which the *true* value of life has faded in favor of material gain, monetary worth, and striving for the tangibles. Too many have lost perspective and our society is preoccupied with things that are really not important in the full picture. Where has all the caring gone? What has happened to man *really* helping man? As long as there are people, there will be caring. But it is limited, small in scope, nothing like it is supposed to be.

Our emphasis in life needs to be redirected. Accept life for what was intended! Make it a total learning experience—every second of every day. Let no day go by without something positive, because there is something positive in every day. Make each day count—your life is but a countdown!

Inspiration is a 4-letter word—*LIFE!!*

Consider Me Read From Finish To Start

Why would you still ask the questions?
If the answers are already known,
Would you be destined to live the same way?
If you know your life's destiny,

Would you still travel that same road?
If you know what lies at the end of the road,
Could you live life as a game of Jeopardy?
Should you live life as a game of Jeopardy?

Would that be equally challenging?
Do we live with trying to figure the questions?
So how significant is coping with what happened first?
Living the finish first removes the mystery,

Where is life's challenge if the answers are known?
Would there be even a need for instant replay?
How could instant replay be used, if at all?
Would changing after the fact change anything?

Could you in fact live your life in reverse?
Would anything change if you know the answer?
How would you live if you know the result?
When beginning is the end and end the beginning,

By living from end to beginning?
Can you visualize living your life
Then start is finish and finish start.
If this is read from finish to start,

Coping

Cope with all that surrounds you
 On a level that will give
  Positive feelings about things
  In your life that are
   Not satisfying but what
   God intended

Cope also with the satisfying
 Or pleasant things that happen
  Perhaps teaching you the
    Importance of all of life and
    Not just what you think
    God intended

Cope with tragedy and pleasure equally
 On the hope that you gain that
  Promise to eternal life
   In a way leading you to
   Not deny what
    God intended

Coping with Life

Much of our lives is centered around coping
We have to cope with others at work and play
We have to cope with "crazies" on the roads
We have to cope with our children daily
And, if we have one, our spouse
If we don't succeed as hoped, we have to cope with failure
If we do succeed, we must cope with success
Growing up, we had to cope with the "loves" we lost
We all, at times, have to cope with grief
Losing someone close, through death, requires extreme coping
Some of us must cope with a physical impairment
Or when we find a sickness that will not leave

But how do we cope with true love lost
What do we do once we find and then lose
Coping with that compounds all the other coping we must do
As with dealing with death, it is ongoing, never-ending
It will not abate but, at times, will tend to worsen
How do we face the fact the other no longer wants us
No longer wants to be with us, or do things with us
What must we do to adjust our lives in order to cope
How do we deal with the daily events we must face
How do we hide what we feel when dealing with others
How do we control what we feel when we are alone
We ask, why does life have to be that way

Maybe it's that way to help us strengthen
Maybe it's that way to test our strength
Maybe it's that way to watch us cope
Maybe it's that way just because it is life
So here we sit coping with life.

Life Questions

Where does life's "secret" lie
Where is the true answer
> Is there truly a "secret"
> Is the answer obvious

Must we spend our lives searching
Must we seek reasons for existing
> Why do we go thru all this
> Why is our time here necessary

Is the answer so simple
Is the reason "just because"
> Did life only just happen
> Did someone/something put us here

Will the answer ever be known
Will those left see the truth
> What happened to cause all this
> What will cause the "discovery"

Is perpetual survival possible
Is life destined to end
> Why must this secret continue
> Why can we not be shown

Are we supposed to find out
Are we expected to continue searching
> Is there life after life
> Is this it

Ken Hanna

Life itself means questions
Our destiny is in part to ask
We must search thru life alone
And we must search with another
The ultimate is the searching
The answer lies in the looking
Life's truth is not for us to know
We will discover it "Next Time."

Continue Being

Why do we search this life?
To find ourselves—
To seek who we are—
Or just to find answers?
When we cannot find what we want,
Do we stop looking?
Certainly not!
Our search is part of our being;
If we stop searching, we stop being!
When we stop being, we begin just existing.
And our lives are more than just existence.
How can we afford to waste today?
We cannot!
Our search must continue;
It can never stop.
But we must accept all we find,
And learn—
For what is the worth in searching
If we cannot learn from what we find?
We must try to find ourselves,
And who we are,
But accept all answers.
Continue the search—Continue being!

—Reprinted from *My Life and Times*

Ken Hanna

Is Our Past Gone?

In the stilled darkness of Spring's first night
The perspective of my outlook is cleared
To the point that I can reconcile the questions in my mind
And see the problems in a new light
To view my life as it has been and now is
To see where I have been and better where I am headed
We know the past is past and not to be relived
But the memories of our past can be relived in our dreams
The good and bad we have felt should be remembered
Our past is ours alone and we must treasure it
The growing, the hurts, the joys, the loves—all of it
What we have had is ours anytime we want it
Treasured in our minds—available at any call
But to recall our past is to recall an experience
An experience that is useful in the present
For coping with the future
To remember what we learned will help us now
And strengthen us for what will come
But not to the point that we try to live in the past
For what is past—has passed!
We must live in the now to grow for the yet to come—
Our past is sacred but not to the point of worship
Live now for now
Do not let your "life" dominate you
You are the control—
You make of it what you will
The future can only be great!

Reprinted from *My Life and Times*

Imagination's Reality

Lives are built on dreams
  -Dreams about what was
    —About what is
      —About what might be

Dreams of our desires
  -Of images of ourselves
    —Of our needs
      —Of perceived success

We "find" recognition
  -Wanted changes in our lives
    —Desire of another's love
      —Even dreams of death

Dreams are imagination's reality
  -And we all imagine
    —We reconcile the "bad"
      —We enhance the "good"

We can resolve problems
  -We maintain the past
    —Relationships gone are not forgotten
      —Those dead are kept "alive"

Keep your dreams
  -Never stop imagining
    —Continue remembering
      —Dream to Reality—

To Ponder Life

To sit in our room alone to ponder,
To try to reason our existence,
Is what we do to answer this wonder,
As we fight defeat and all resistance.

We try to explain why we are here,
And the purpose God intended,
In part so we can face all fear,
And fight those obstacles 'till they're ended.

We all search for that happy life,
And hope that problems will not find us,
But we must learn to face all strife,
So that what we find will not destroy us.

If we are to maintain any hope,
That there is a life after death,
We should teach ourselves how to cope,
And fulfill our lives with every breath.

We are here to prepare and train,
For what we are yet to be,
As God has made us face the pain,
So our total life we can better see.

Once we can see what lies ahead,
And we know what God has planned,
That when we die we're not dead,
We must place ourselves in His hand.

So keep your faith and always pray,
Your life is happy and complete,
And it surely will be every day,
Then all is yours and eternity you'll meet.

—Reprinted from *My Life and Times*

Life Is

Life is but what it is
　　Nothing less but so much more

Life is not explained in words
　　It is a feeling and emotion

Life is a certain state of mind
　　A sense of what we are

Life is our testing ground
　　Or moment in which to practice

Life is linked confrontations
　　One challenge leading to another

Life is combined experiences
　　A test of our reactions

Life is love versus hate
　　Our time to choose a path

Life is acceptance of death
　　A chance to anticipate Eternity

Life is a coping process
　　How will we use our time

Life is momentary existence
　　That fragment He has allowed

Life is but what it is

That Breath of Life

As I lay on Mother Earth with my eyes to the sky
    I saw Heaven open Her doors so my mind could fly
felt a rush and resurgence that I have not felt
    And without a hesitation all my sorrows did melt

There, with outstretched arms, my angel welcomed me
    And I immediately sensed the true meaning of "free"
Her smile melted all sadness that lived in my heart
    I knew forever hence a new happiness would start

With but a look, she showed me how precious is all of life
    That its last breath is the first breath of Eternal Life
When we each take that breath, a new stage will be set
    So this life need be lived with a heart cleansed of fret

Ken Hanna

Adventure to Adventure

Adventure relates to Adventure
The lesson of each will prepare us
For the next yet to be experienced
The relationship may not always be obvious
But the fact that we learned a lesson
Makes us better prepared in accepting each
That in itself would relate all adventures
We are given our lives for one reason
To make of them what we will
And since we all will experience adventures
Our lives too must be interrelated
We therefore should learn from those with whom
    we come in contact
As well as from our own adventures
Do not take for granted any part of life
Be it our own or someone else's
Our lives are our total being
Our lives are why we are here
Our lives are all we have
Our lives are incomplete without adventures
The more adventures the more complete our lives
The more complete our lives the better prepared
Prepared for our next beginning
What is now and yet to be.

—Reprinted from *My Life and Times*

The Breath of Life

With each breath that I would take
I sense the joy that lies ahead
For life's bounty let us forsake
What we would feel from our dread

To allow each moment to be fulfilled
With all that comes from the Creation
Love's justification has been willed
And we can feel all life's elation

So waste not a moment of your time
For the moment now will soon pass
To create an aura of all that's sublime
And the pleasure itself will forever last

To yourself and to others be but kind
Embrace life's moments tight to your breast
Store every experience within your mind
So when life's over you can peacefully rest

Ken Hanna

Reward for Experience

As we grow we face many situations
Often too numerous to mention
Often too hard to handle
Often too traumatic to live with
But we continue
Continue to fight
Continue to struggle
Continue to grow
We try love
We test love
And love tests us
That test is often great
And all too often it proves too great
But we must face all challenges
So survival is foremost
We need to look beyond the present
Around the corner will be another destiny
The anticipation in itself should keep us going
But how do we confront each destiny
How do we meet these challenges
For every minute of every day is a challenge
And as soon as we realize that things will be easier
Not easier to accept
Not easier to handle
Only easier to cope with
Cope and Continue
Learn and Grow
We should confront each destiny with a certain attitude
An attitude that will allow us to look beyond the surface
To search for a reason why
Why this destiny has touched us
For everything has a reason
When we sort the reason we can face the challenge

118

We do not control our destiny
But we can affect it
Affect it by our approach to it
By our attitude about it
By our reasoning for it
Each confrontation is but an experience
And each experience is a teacher
Someone to learn from
Someone to help us find the way
Not just the way but the path to follow
To help us hopefully follow the right way
To face each roadblock head-on
Meet it—Confront it—Continue by it.

—Reprinted from *My Life and Times*

The Good and Grim

Love your life—it's all you have
The alternative is quite dim.
'Tho life will test us every day
Accept the good and all the grim.

Be humble when the good arrives
Be strong when the grim should come.
Always trust the tests you're given
They are for all not just for some.

Realize all of life cannot be easy
The true test comes when you face strife.
You learn to work thru all the agony
That is the real challenge in your life.

The good is very easy to accept
Your elation makes you beam so bright.
We all want only joyous times
A happy life with shining lights.

But your fate is to experience hurt
And all the necessary pain.
The resolve comes in accepting that
You appreciate better what you attain.

How Good Is Bad/How Bad Is Good

When it comes to life, we are all so frail
    We face new obstacles each time we fail

But to fail is necessary to fulfill our life
    As life's incomplete without times of strife

Ignoring struggles will make life seem longer
    But facing problems makes our faith stronger

Accept the fact that problems will always exist
    And they hurt more when you choose to resist

Try to find a positive in all the bad you face
    For when you do, the negative you can erase

How can you know the true value of any good
    But confront the bad, it's what you should

Keep good in perspective, as well as all bad
    For the time you are given, you will be glad

No matter what, lose not love for yourself ever
    For self-love will provide contentment forever.

To Be Happy in Life

'Tho life poses challenges at every turn,
We must not shy but face them head on.
Happiness is a goal for which we all yearn,
But too often it comes after we're gone.

Whatever this life has in store for us all,
Our acceptance of that will give us peace.
And help will come from memories we recall,
To give us strength and let hate be released.

Only happiness will give us that frame of mind,
So we can better accept adversities that come.
Love all people the same and always be kind,
For we know not from where happiness will come.

Treat all you would meet in the same way,
And never carry hatred within your heart.
Take time to ask for help whenever you pray,
For when that's done your happy life will start.

Giving

Splendid indeed is this life we can live
Think of the capacity we have to just give

So why do so many feel we must always take
That we make that choice and giving forsake

We have the chance to choose one or the other
Why so often do we choose to take from another

The rewards we gain from giving can be so grand
And there is no greater joy in all of the land

So why not try soon this simple act of giving
You'll discover you hadn't really been living

What a joy you will find entering your heart
An elation so incomparable setting it apart

Be alive and give—give and you will be alive
For all you want, for this you should strive

It is such an easy task for all of us to do
So why are the numbers who try but so few

Think what a greater world could be created
A peaceful world for which all have waited

Just imagine if only one more would simply try
The effect would snowball—for joy would God cry!

—And Yet

As I peer thru the window, what is it I see
Past the thick, hazy air is the shadow of a tree
'Tho I cannot see it, I know the sky is still there
    —And yet the onset of Spring shows life still bare

The rejuvenation is in waiting to open once more
To blossom forth, the rekindling of life to pour
The time for love to grow will again begin its charge
    —And yet life's purpose remains for us large

We are reminded of why we are in existence here
That our strength of faith will tamp down our fear
This is our time when tomorrow's hope is so sure
    —And yet life as we know is our chance to be pure

We see how fragile is life and how we are so frail
That for our time we say thanks and without fail
To live our moment the fullest we possibly can
    —And yet know life goes on as when time began

Your Eternity Will Survive

An eternal life can truly be at hand.
It could spread throughout the land.
If only more would want to strive,
We would all feel so much more alive.
Given the chance then more would try,
"But life is too tough," is the reply.

If not for that, then why are we here?
To value eternity, we must have fear!
Facing that fact is too hard for some,
But to accept it means it will come.
It matters not whatever you believe.
Just believe and you can conceive!

Think how you feel when you do good.
You will be elated just as you should.
It's a harder life when you carry hate.
Hate in your heart—eternity will wait!
Hate will make you flounder each day.
Replace it with love—for that, pray!

Life is endless with love in your heart,
But tomorrow's too late for a new start.
Today's the day when eternity will be set;
You'll feel the force when goodness is met.
The rush you get makes you feel so alive.
A heart of love—eternity will survive!

Your Time Is Now

So short is your time and is your life—
But a fraction of all that has been
You're given blends of good with strife—
Then count not what you do but when

Too many say that tomorrow is the day—
They feel they have time on their side
But tomorrow comes and it is now today—
And replaces yesterday as the day to bide

Realize your time allowed is not known—
You must say that your time is here
Your time provided is all that's shown—
That it will end is what you must fear

Fear not the end because it's the end—
But fear your time that you do not know
Cling to faith is the message God sends—
And time well spent is the image you show

Do not let the sad dwell in your mind—
Let the happy prevail for your given time
Go not thru life with eyes that are blind—
Live with glad moments and do not whine

The time of your life is just being alive—
And each moment down will draw you away
When love prevails your memory will survive—
For contentment again is what you should pray.

Live - Not Exist

Let your heart and mind control your life
    Instill love so it will live in both
        Value all the good that lives around you
        Enjoy the rewards that will come

Never let hate take over your feelings
    Only allow peaceful thoughts to exist
        Try to fulfill God's wish for you

Experience the wonder that abounds in life
    X-tol the virtue of a joyful existence
        Initiate those feelings that will give peace
        Savor the elation of life that awaits
        Taste of life—not just exist

Ken Hanna

Accept What He Intended

I lie in my bed and dream of death,
Of life itself and my every breath.
Why has He caused me all this pain,
Is His purpose clouded or simply plain?

Am I challenged to deal with strife,
What is meant for me in this life?
Must I face grief during all my years,
Or will happiness come and wipe my tears?

The miracle of life twice came to me,
Blessed extensions for my eternity.
I see my memory as living on,
For now and long after I am gone.

We all desire to be known forever,
Recalled in thought not vanished ever.
We lay the path as we'll be known,
For those behind need to be shown.

The choice is ours of the life we lay,
For some it's clear and for many it's gray.
We think we see what God drew for us,
Often denying it as seeming unjust.

So we try to change what seems our fate,
And carry in our hearts unneeded hate.
His intent was to have only love exist,
But frailties have caused us to resist.

Our purpose should be to accept His plan,
Reconcile our faith and take His hand.
Let Him guide us as He knows how,
Through life's trials we must start now.

Self-Esteem In Life

See yourself in a mirrored image
Expect the best as you would see it
Learn your attributes and your faults
Focus on your entire self!

    Exemplify that personality as imagined
    Set your sights on the best you can be
    Take all your ability to the highest limit
    Exclude the negatives from your mind
    Expect the most from what you have
    Make your life "count"!

Include all the positives you can find
Notice all the good around you!

    Learn to avoid that which hurts you
    Instill a feeling of warmth about you
    Feel the essence of what He made you
    Enjoy yourself for who you are!

From Night To Light

'Tho life for all is but a valued treasure
Been given to us to provide us pleasure
Too many take its purpose for granted
Because the seed to know was never planted

Life holds for us all countless wonders
We stand in awe these treasured wonders
Who with such infinite wisdom created all
So this total creation upon us did fall

Should not our quest be knowledge first
Knowledge allows us to satisfy our thirst
We enter with innate desire to know why
For all our days that endless quest we try

But when will the answer be ever shown
Will truth be evident and eternally known
Will this mystery finally come to light
So forever our days will never see night

Reach Not That Light

Loneliness of each day reaches to encompass me
It takes hold and increasingly squeezes tightly
I fight the grasp but too often cannot release
A feeling of drowning swallows my thoughts
I think tomorrow will never come to me

I see this day for which I am not ready
The days have melted together, no longer distinct
Each becomes just as every other—not individual
Just as one ends another lies ready to begin
I do not look forward as I always did before

Knowing the next one will imitate those before
I think, what is the point to continue anew
What I will experience I have already faced
The challenge of a rewarding day is no longer there
Boredom and depression have set their marks on me

Significant marks which only overwhelm me
Fighting those feelings seems a losing battle
It seems I am becoming totally engulfed
Getting swallowed and devoured, losing identity
Feeling aloneness must be the ultimate emptiness

Love and friendship have departed my being
Those I leaned on have not seen me reach out
So I sit alone in stillness to ponder tomorrow
When tomorrow comes, will I be here to welcome it
Or will I be elsewhere with a new beginning

My waning years confirm the tunnel's light
Do I reach out to touch that light
Or do I wait for the natural arrival
My faith tells me the days will again separate
The natural progression should be allowed

Belief in tomorrow can never be destroyed
My depression and loneliness will tomorrow pass
The tunnel's light will have to wait for me
I will reach it when God has intended
This has been His challenge for me

I have faced His challenge and accepted it
The severest test I have ever faced
A test that wins each battle but not the war
I cannot let the war end for me yet
Giving in only shows weakness has won

So I must fight that weakness each day
And show God I will wear it down
Cause it to fade and eventually vanish
Tomorrow will bring me a new strength
Not always tomorrow but maybe the next tomorrow

I must wait and fight, that is my faith
Something in each day must give me strength
I look towards tomorrow for renewed faith
For I know God made sure it will be there
That light will not touch me until He intended.

Ken Hanna

A Question of Dying

I feel self-pity—
    Why did this happen to me?
I feel regret—
    Why did I not do more with my life?
I feel remorse—
    Why can't I undo the bad I've done?
I feel urgency—
    Why only six months; that is not enough time?
I feel depression—
    Why does my remaining time have to cause me grief?
I feel pain—
    Why does impending death have to be a painful time?
I feel failure—
    Why couldn't I have been better, so this may not have
    happened?
I feel afraid—
    Why am I so scared of dying?

    Will I be drawn by that Light?
    Will I be allowed into Heaven?
    Will I become an angel?
    Will I spend time or forever in Hell for my sins?
    Will I be allowed to observe those left behind?
    Will I "live" in eternal bliss?
    Will I spend eternity with those who preceded me?
    Will I finally get answers to all my questions?

To die is why we all live
To die is how we gain eternal life
To die is the "remedy" for having been here
To die is the solution to the question of life
To die is what we all must accept
To die is how we will gain true contentment
To die is to mean we will always live
To die is what it is all about

The Promise of Life

Tears well up as I sit here all alone
I see my past as loneliness sets the tone
There have been happy times during my years
But the sad times are heightened by my tears

It's a moment when I'm controlled by sad
And I must set aside the good I have had
Everyone has known those times of despair
And we feel that life has been unfair

We all deal with woes in a different way
Some will run and some will try to pray
Some will cower and some will get depressed
Some will end it all and some will just regress

We must learn first what life is all about
To understand pain that will make us shout
Our first thoughts say it will never end
And our broken heart will never mend

But you tell yourself that that is not true
Life will get better just as the sky is blue
Happiness will return as God meant it should
Tomorrow will be good as He promised it would.

Eternal Peace Is at Hand

With your head held high, much can be done
All the rewards you desire can then be won
Life itself is a challenge for all to face
Good or bad, there is nothing it will replace
Our time spent here is but a time of trial
So accept that fact and live not with denial

You can make living easy or make it tough
But just coasting through life is not enough
You must take charge of this time you spend
Rely not on others —only on your faith depend
Live all your life with but love in your heart
When God sees that, your eternity will start

You will not enter Heaven if you carry any hate
And your eternal peace will then have to wait
We all will ultimately have to answer to Him
And if we show hate, our eternity will look dim
So work always hard to rid hate from your mind
Then that eternal peace you will surely find.

Ken Hanna

How Is Time to Be Spent

The time is here as I look thru the snow's glisten;
And, Lo, I hear a voice and am compelled to listen.

Its sound is so softening as it mellows my heart—
Pacifying my anxiousness is the effect it imparts!

I have reached a point where questions have occurred,
And all those answers of tomorrow cannot be deferred.

There is need to resolve those questions in my mind,
For I have searched so very long for answers to find.

But do we ever truly find what it is that we seek?
Must we live our days never questioning—just meek?

Everyone wonders, at times, why are we even here?
Was the intent to challenge how we deal with fear?

How many spend this time only worrying about dying,
And wasting our moment simply fretting and crying?

Is finding the purpose of life the challenge we got?
For that to be our only destiny, I would think not!

The faith we must develop tells us what lies ahead—
Of a golden tomorrow filled with love, not dread.

That new beginning will be a contented existence—
An eternity of happiness with no hate or resistance.

For what was meant to be, our faith says will be.
Our life now is but a cleansing for our eternity.

So waste not time trying to change what's been set!
Accept what you're given—a happier life will be met!

My Life Fulfilled

I saw my dreams before me rise
    And all at once I knew
My feelings and my thoughts reprised
    Sorrowed times were through

I knew the times that lay ahead
    Would culminate my life
That joy had spoken and what it said
    Was live all free of strife

So now I face each of my days
    On only the joyous side
Of soaring wings held up by praise
    Until all memory's died

I see my life as been complete
    And fulfilled with love
My satisfaction is totally replete
    I will observe from above

Lo, let my words be your guide
    To fulfill your needs
On those wings you too will glide
    With words from thoughtful creeds

How?

How great the struggle
   from day to day—
      Constantly fighting life
      for survival—

How easy it is to just quit
   and give in to it all—
      The struggle is overwhelming
      and appears winless—

How do we continue and
   fight off the stress—
      Can we cope with it
      for a chance at tomorrow—

How great this life when we
   give it a chance—
      All we need to prove that
      is consider the alternative—

How strong must we be
   to keep our hope alive—
      Where must we turn
      when our faith is tested—

How is it our lives
   must have hurt at all—
      Why cannot life itself
      be filled with happiness—

Ken Hanna

How can happiness be enjoyed
with nothing to compare—
For life to be savoured
good and bad must exist—

How good will be the good
lest we experience bad—
To know the bad will happen
should be our preparation—

Is Alone Lonely?

How lonely is life when we are alone!
Depression is felt by all we are shown.
We feel we are lost with nowhere to go;
No one is there; life has lost its glow.
Where do we turn, and what will we do?
Is tomorrow better or is life through?

Our faith cannot fade for us to survive.
We must strengthen our hope to stay alive.
The easy out is to just quit and give in;
But to quit now means we can never win!
We see the struggle lost; continue we must.
Put aside all pity, and go on without fuss!

Trust that God will provide us a better day.
Know tomorrow gets better, so hope and pray!
We all must be alone at some time in life;
To renew our beliefs, and tamp down strife.
So being alone need not mean being lonely.
Nothing beyond no one around, it is that only!

The Pain in Loneliness

Through the stilled silence of loneliness
    I hear the pain of being alone—
It provides time for contemplation
    Time to reflect on my past—
To look ahead to a possible future
    And to evaluate where my present lives—
It appears I have traveled full-circle
    I have felt complete happiness—

True contentment was in my life
    I have had the pain of lost love—
Found love anew and lost again
    My present lives in bewilderment—
I cannot completely realize where I am
    But mostly I know not where I am headed—
I am not able to identify what I now want
    It just gets harder to see my tomorrow—

Loneliness can be a fatal disease
    It can grow like a malignant infection—
It will swallow rationalization
    And destroy the ability to reason—
Loneliness can drain your strength to fight
    Sad are the numbers who have given in—
Those who lost the faith to continue the fight
    What could have laid ahead for them—

144

How might their futures have turned
    No one knows but for them alone—
Recognize that to give up means to finalize
    The moment next will never be felt—
Let curiosity and faith always prevail
    Know that life is but continuous change—
What is this moment will not be the next
    What is sad today will pass tomorrow—

Our lives are but glad and sad blended
    Not one has lived without some pain—
But know that night gives way to day
    And pain clears the soul for the next joy—
Live your life for all experience
    Do not ever let life live for you—
Let faith keep you here for tomorrow
    For tomorrow is yet a new life—

It's Good/It's Bad/It's Life

How demoralizing can our given time be,
As you think to yourself, "God, why me?"
You make efforts with your head held high,
But to continue on, you must always try.
Do not even consider ever giving in,
Because once you've lost, you'll never win.

Seek our strength wherever it may be,
And hope will ensue as you will see.
Your challenges in life will never abate,
But don't let setbacks create a hate.
Accept what life has in store for you,
For each day will set a test anew.

Know the downside that life will provide,
Then much of the pain you'll see subside.
Be humble when life for you has been good,
For rewards will increase as they should.
Good and bad are the sum total of life;
The joys we get as well as the strife.

Accept that fact and you will ease the pain;
Use all the joy for the strength you'll gain.
When hurt arrives, that strength is there
To get you through when life's been "unfair."
So keep all your faith and do not let go;
It will see you through as the joy will grow!

The Seasons of Life

Without fail, the seasons take their turns
Each one providing its own life of challenges
Challenges that often dare us to fold and give up
Barriers put up to block what could be happiness
Walls against any possible contentment
Our strength is pummeled and weakened

Causing never-ending conflict within our minds
Why must life be so difficult and complex
Why cannot "this" life be peaceful and happy
Simply, this life is our training ground
Spring is the seed representing all life
It is the budding onset of life old and new

All new life begins now from a planted seed
And old life is rejuvenated to begin anew
Summer is the nourishment of all life
As Spring is the conception, Summer is the blossoming
The sun's vital rays mixed with the rain's feeding
All life grows, strengthens, and becomes content

Autumn provides the waning moments before the end
Life destined to end begins its preparation
Preparation for the long "rest" is started
Death is gradual and the selection is begun
Winter now becomes the culmination of the cycle
What life is to end will now fulfill its destiny

The selection determined for the coming onset
And then all life will begin again
As we see our lives is set in Spring
We plan our happiness and our purpose
What our lives will be and how we will fulfill the Dream
Living that Dream and purpose will that Summer be

How long our Summer will last is not known to us
So we must strive for satisfaction of the Dream
Autumn warns us that our "time" is near
There is but little time for our fulfillment
But this is not time for worry or regrets
We have had our time and we must say "thanks"

It is time to prepare for our next stage
Let peace and contentment enter our minds
Winter arrives and so on we move
Move to that next stage and make room
For the new cycle lies just ahead of us
Our purpose for being will now end

But our reason should live on with the next cycle
The seed of new life must contain our reason
Through memories we can continue to "live"
Our lives will change as surely as do the seasons
And that will be our cycle of life
But our lives will continue to "live" the seasons of life.

Winter Time

Winter's snow has vanished and with it the glisten
The season of life has turned it depressing gray
I hear not sounds of nature, yet I continue to listen
Why have all living things gone rather than stay

Do they know that Winter is a connotation of Death
And their continued survival rests but with rest
Time for rejuvenation of strength and renewed breath
Time to reflect and plan with infirmities repressed

It is our time, too, to look back with great heed
To previous times, how has our life been altered
Have we lived with but love or with hate and greed
Did we recognize mistakes at those times we faltered

Now we must prepare ourselves for the ensuing Spring
The moment new love is expected to blossom and bloom
That time when nature returns and the birds will sing
When all will grow with the cycle of Winter coming soon

So Winter now must be used by all of us to prepare
We, like all of nature, need contemplation and rest
To weigh our lives—all good and bad to each compare
Confront all problems—then face head-on Winter's test

So understand and accept God's chance for all of us
As each new Winter should be used for what He intended
Think, reflect, and plan for better and without a fuss
Make the gray of Winter a time you have but befriended.

Where Am I Going

Thy wings did float on lofty breeze
    My soul was peaced and calmly eased
A sense of value I finally met
    No more troubled days I have to fret

From days gone by 'till time to come
    I know where my fate came from
To where my journey will lead me now
    I remain forever humble with wrinkled brow

I will treat all of life as if my own
    Until my day to Heaven I have flown
And there I meet where all began
    To see for myself the Original Plan

So the days I've left I will enjoy
    And that path to happiness I will employ
Now guide me wings to my Eternal Home
    Then forever more I may roam

When I Die

When I die I want Heaven
When I die I want Life
    I want to see all who went before
    I want to say what was never said
        When I Die

Will dying be the end of it
Will dying be the new beginning
    I hope for death to be a start
    I hope for death to bring new life
        When I Die

I am not afraid to know I'm dying
I am not about to panic
    What is to be will be
    What is to happen will happen
        When I Die

To know I'm dying is a blessing
To know I'm dying lets me prepare
    Fear of death will block preparation
    Fear of death will affect my faith
        When I Die

When I die my life's complete
When I die then will I live
    I know there is a God and Heaven
    I know there is a place for me
        When I Die

My Senses Enlightened

I asked God did I savour a Heavenly taste
A joy and pleasure that was a sin to waste
And then I arose with my fears to be faced
    —All His wonderful peace was I finally graced

Then God I asked pray what did He feel
Lo, His hands touched me and felt so real
Thy strength was so deep my soul I felt heal
    —So great was I comforted as my fate did seal

When I asked God to tell what did He see
I felt His eyes as they totally engulfed me
And with that did I find myself feel so free
    —I knew then what awaited was my Eternity

I asked Him the aroma that it was I did smell
Because it gave me a sense of feeling so well
My mind filled with thoughts I wanted to tell
    —That sweet fragrance made my excitement swell

And then I asked Him whatever did He hear
As I heard a voice of love within mine ear
It gave me such peace and took away my fear
    —His words simply told me He was always near

Hands of Love

When I looked up, with my eyes in awe
I felt a gentle touch, a hand did draw
And it beckoned me in my mind's eye
To see what I had not, to feel that sigh

My thoughts were formed and I saw love
That hand of fate reached me from above
And the touch I felt was strong but kind
It gave me comfort, my soul was entwined

That comforting peace was inside of me
And all of my burdens I did finally free
No longer will this life be on me a strain
For now I know all eternity I will gain

I felt that hand on my shoulder did show
How simply love can make all life grow
Our moment here is but a speck of sand
Thy destiny we expect is ours to command

I am now forever with this life at peace
All troubles and sorrows I have released
So I will set sail toward that Eternal Love
Guided by that hand that touched from above

Where Is Heaven, Anyway?

Is this Heaven, where does it lie—
Is it here, or beyond the sky—
Is Heaven everywhere, or just in our mind—
Can it be something we will someday find—
Is Heaven a place that will stand alone—
Is it a place we will call home—
　　Where is Heaven, anyway?

Will we get there on a cloud of white—
Will the sun still shine so bright—
Will this life be the end of it all—
Can we bring our memories to recall—
Will love exist as we know it here—
Will hate disappear along with fear—
　　Where is Heaven, anyway?

What will we do for continued existence—
What about obstacles and resistance—
What happens if this life is the end—
Can we touch our family and friends—
What of the eternity to be spent—
What truly was God's real intent—
　　Where is Heaven, anyway?

Thy Hands-Of-Eight

I dreamed I touched thy hands-of-eight;
And asked my Lord, "What is my fate?"

What means these hands, outstretched to me?
Are they the hands of destiny?

Are they Thine hands from up above;
Sent to carry me on wings of love?

Why only hands and not the eyes
To pierce my soul, cause it to rise?

Why not a voice that speaks my name?
Just hands outstretched, from whence they came?

I pray thee, Lord, what means these hands
That beckon me from distant lands?

These hands that flutter like the breeze,
That waft so gently thru the trees.

And God replied in gentle tone,
"These hands I sent for you, alone.

To bring you to my pearly gate,
This task assigned to hands-of-eight."

And I did ask, with head bowed low,
"This then does mean that I must go?"

And God replied in words divine,
"Yes, My son, you now are Mine."

Ken Hanna

A Blended Life

Day passes into Night
    And Night reciprocates
The one complements the other
    A perfect blend of extremes

With no possible variations

Would that our lives could mimic
    But such a Life
Filled only with variations
    Each moment different

Hopefully blended with another

And the worth of our lives
    Judged by the mix provided
Lives are filled with unmixables
    Those determine our worth

These are basic to our character

Some are confronted with many
    Some are faced with few
All of us are met with some
    Together with the mixables

A blend of moments of experience

A combination of good and bad
    A mix of happy and sad
Humbly accepting the mixables
    Makes unmixables tolerable

Experiences melt into an olio

Good can lead to bad
    Happy can be turned to sad
A recipe of our lives
    Simply a combination of ingredients

Blended together and called LIFE

My Wish To You

May you be blessed with all that you want in life
May all the dreams you have forever come true
May peace and contentment remain your foundation
May love fill your heart as it does for but a few.

Let your heart guide you over the right path
Let God fill you with His everlasting love
Let health and happiness continue to exist in you
Let life's rewards come down from above.

Be at peace within you through your years
Be grateful for whatever would come your way
Be generous and helpful to all who would need them
Be satisfied in all of life, for that you should pray.

Learn to handle what you can and cannot do
Learn to love all parts of your life
Learn to accept the frailties in all of us
Learn to cope with the negatives of life.

Look for the positive side in all experiences
Look for the good that exists in everyone
Look for God's answer to all you question
Look for the faith you need to continue on.

Find the peaceful path to follow throughout
Find the satisfaction that lies in wait for you
Find the love that will let you cope with Life
Find the joy that God intended for you.

About the Author

Ken, an Indiana native, has had careers in teaching/coaching, accounting, insurance, office management because he has challenged himself to constantly learn. Writing has always been his "personal" therapist. He is also the author of *Thoughts From a Mind That Never Rests*—a compilation of original and inspirational quotes. Ken has published these books with the hope they can help others looking for answers to the trials of life or to just feel some inspiration at chosen moments.

Printed in the United States
4763